TALES AND TRAILS: A WESTERN ODYSSEY

CREATIVE QUILLS WRITING GROUP

Creative Quills Publishing Group
El Reno, OK

Copyright 2016 by Creative Quills
All Rights Reserved.

No part of this book may be reproduced by any mechanical, photographic, or electronic process, or in the form of a phonographic recording; nor may it be stored in a retrieval system, transmitted, or otherwise copied for public or private use—other than for "fair use" as brief quotations embodied in articles and reviews—without prior written permission of the author/publisher.

The stories in this book are works of fiction. All of the characters, names, incidents, dialogue, and many of the locales are works from the author's imagination or are places used fictitiously. Any resemblance to people living or dead is purely coincidental.

Cover design: Andrea Foster
Front Cover photo: Sue D. L. Smith
Back Cover photo: Chuck Baker

ISBN- 13: 978-0692803653
ISBN-10:0692803653

This book is dedicated to
all the folks at CVTech who have aided us
in our writing and publishing dreams!
These include Neil Blitzer, Karen Sneary,
Josh Shandy, Kari Mulligan,
and the other staff members
who are always there for us!

INDEX

Introduction	9
Forward	11
PJ Acker	13
Chuck Baker	25
Alicia Ballard	37
Judy Bishop	43
Glenda Brown	57
Alton "Tuna" Dobbins	81
Rosemarie Durgin	101
Debbie Fogle	111
Andrea Foster	127
Carol Gimbel	147
Woody Gimbel	155
Johnna Kaye	171
Bernadette Lowe	187
Julie Marquardt	203
Carol Nichols	217
Shane Smith	233
Sue D. L. Smith	251
Hart Tillett	265
Acknowledgements	281

INTRODUCTION

In fall of 2014, I approached Neil Blitzer, adult class coordinator of the Canadian Valley Vocational Center with an idea to offer a class called Write Publish & Market Your Book. I had been in the book business in one form or another for most of my life, and since many people ask me for my help on a regular basis, I thought, *Why not?* Neil agreed, and we scheduled offerings for the Winter/Spring semester of 2015. To promote the classes, I went into the El Reno Carnegie Library that January 2015 to ask if I could post a flyer about them. Serendipitously, Library Director Amy Brandley was at the main desk, and she graciously accepted to post my flyer and spread the word.

A week or so later, Amy contacted me again to ask if I would be interested in leading some writing classes for Poetry Month in April at the library. I said, "Sure!" We set a date, and the Creative Quills Writing Group at the El Reno Carnegie Library was born.

Once Poetry Month was over, we kept on going! We explored our creativity of the written word through writer's prompts, writing to music and pictures, and "pot luck" picking of characters, plots, and scenarios.

We created heroes and villains, made chapbooks and broadsides, participated in National Novel Writing Month, had a writer's booth at the El Reno Burger Day Festival, and recently published a book of short stories called *Alternate Perspectives*, based on a writer's exercise we shared.

We are a busy little group, and we live off instant inspiration and each other's creative sparks! This book is a result of that. This summer, I revisited reading the book *Lonesome Dove* by Larry McMurtry, and I asked the group, "How about we write some Westerns?" They were all up for the challenge! This book is the result of the vision and creativity of our writer's group Creative Quills. We hope you enjoy reading as much as we enjoy writing!

Andrea Foster, Group Leader and Editor

FORWARD

The old West was wild and fraught with danger. Greenhorn settlers, tinhorn gamblers, ruthless gunslingers, crooked law men, and dance hall floozies mixed with robbers, riders, posses, padres, storekeepers, blacksmiths, bankers, robber barons, and ne'er-do-wells. In this book, you'll ride stagecoaches down dusty trails to frontier settlements desperately needing law and order, medicine to fight disease, and common decency. These stories attempt to mix fact and fiction to bring that era to you in the comfort of your air-conditioned home, while waiting for the automatic dryer to finish your laundry, as dinner is in the electric oven, so you can relax in your recliner and enjoy "the good old days". –Chuck Baker, author

PJ ACKER

JACOB'S CHOICE

PJ Acker is an artist and writer with an eye out for the next adventure while living in the land of many tornados. She loves writing, painting, kayaking, biking and adventures. She lives with her husband and two pushy cats.

JACOB'S CHOICE

by PJ Acker

Waiting was hard.

Crouching in the darkness, Jacob reached down, pulled a blade of grass from the wet ground and began to chew. Wet and chilled from the night's rain, he continued to wait in silence.

Daylight was taking her sweet time. The forest that usually brought him such comfort was providing none tonight.

If it didn't rain through dawn, there'd only be hot vapor by noon. The smothering heat of the Oklahoma summer would come fast on the heels of day's first light, burning off whatever moisture was left by the night rain.

Black was turning to shades of gray. First one by one, then by groups, enormous oaks stepped from the shadows surrounding him like an army of giants—silent accusers, hard and unmoving.

In the distance, lifting from the mist like a ghostly apparition, he could see the old bridge slowly materialize. Resisting a rising panic, Jacob steadied himself. Dragging in a deep breath and spitting grass from his mouth, he rose. It was time.

He moved deliberately, walking through shafts of yellow morning light. Soggy clothes stuck to his body, sending chills as it touched new skin. Dread and hours of stillness made his limbs numb and heavy. From his watch-post overlooking the bridge, he made his slow descent, working numb hands open and closed as he went.

Wading through a low area, fog swirled like a startled animal, twisting around him, trying to hold onto him, as if trying to slow the inevitable. But it couldn't save him. The forest was beginning to stir to life. Jacob remembered the first time he'd brought Molly to the forest, to his special place, and he smiled. Like escapees from a world that never understood, this place had become their refuge. Just over a year ago, it seemed like yesterday. The leaves rustled in the trees overhead. He could hear her laughter soft on the wind. She'd come to love the forest as he did.

A bird's whistle pierced the air sharp and clear. Then several were warbling and calling back and forth. A squirrel scampered through the grass nearby and up a tree trunk. Several frogs began winding up their deep-throated voices and bellowed out loud "croaks". With a sudden stab of memory, nausea rose up in his tight throat. The memory of gentle eyes looking up at him, trusting, loving... the tiniest shadow of something else appeared... something wasn't right. But he didn't want to remember...not yet.

Stepping onto the bridge, he gripped the railing, then lost the battle to keep his mind blank. Squeezing his eyes tight against the memories, images landed like the blows of an angry bat. In his mind he saw afternoon lights dancing patterns across her smiling face. A burgundy dress floated over her soft body.

Memories, like a movie playing through his mind. They'd been best friends, eventually lovers. Midnight rendezvous, playing hooky from school. They never watched the seniors very closely. The ache in his chest deepened. The movie played on.

Leaning over the side of the bridge, his hands felt along the scuffed metal railing where they'd stood. Molly and Jacob's bridge. That's what they'd called it. He could hear echoes of him and Molly laughing, talking, making plans for their future. Like a steel fist, pain and grief gripped him hard as it squeezed the breath from his body.

His eyes darted toward the soft grass next to the

creek, the strap of her sundress sliding from her shoulders revealing soft, perfect skin, smooth and warm. They'd made love. She'd told him she loved him.

Clamping down the memory, desperation rose and he braced himself for what was to come. How could she not love him anymore? The struggle to stop the memories was useless and the scene played on. He could see the tears rolling down her face. He mentally braced himself for what was to come, for the words that would crush him, destroy his world. Heart thumping hard against his chest, he'd been unable to find the words that would change her mind.

Beams of light fell over the grass now, creating odd, distorted shapes that bled across dead ground—across the place where she'd promised to love him, forever. Blowing out an anguished, defeated breath, he could feel the greyness of the morning sliding away. Soon the light would expose what the dark had been hiding.

At the edge of his awareness, something crouched, a hint of something lost, something he should remember, washed away by the gurgling sounds of water splashing over the rocks in the creek below. Not far away, he heard the lonely moan of a loon. Jacob sucked a breath of air, his knees nearly buckling.

Closing his eyes, he breathed deeply, memorizing the smells of the woods: bright, green, fresh—life. The sharp scent of wet pine filled his head, stinging the edges of his nose. He'd always felt at peace here. He'd had a connection to something greater than himself here. It's why he'd brought her here.

The rain was falling in earnest now. From beneath water-soaked hair, through dripping lashes, something caught his eye. On the railing next to his hand, fresh grooves dug into silver paint. Claw marks made from desperate fingernails? A moan escaped his blue lips. He steadied himself once again. I have to finish it, he vowed, his body shaking.

Beneath cold, grief, and exhaustion, a slow rage began to simmer. "But there wasn't any other way!" His strangled confession hissed through clenched teeth as he dropped to the wet bridge.

Like a sharp blade the memory sliced, drawing fresh pain, acute and raw. His attention was riveted to the point of the blade—her sweet, hesitant touches, the sweet sound of her sighs. She did love him once. Acceptance and the grief of her loss drained away all remaining strength. He had no defense now.

From beneath the bridge, he could hear the sound of tires approaching above. A bicycle spinning its way toward the bridge. Thin wheels clamored onto the wooden slats of the old bridge, then stopped. A cautious pause lingered for a moment. Then, in a sudden burst of clattering, he heard the bike being whipped around. Tires bounced back down. Spinning, they finally caught traction. The biker raced back toward the direction from which he'd just come.

"It's been seen! It won't be long now," he sighed. The rain had stopped. He stood staring at the lifeless body that lay on the ground in front of him…in the cool shadows of the bridge. Smells of the damp, dead leaves warming under the Oklahoma sun began to fill the air.

Blood mixed with auburn hair swirled like crimson ribbons above the head as it rested motionless on its pillow of protruding rocks. The yellowed pack and red-checkered shirt would be easy to spot in the light of day.

"Do you think I'll be punished?" he asked. "I mean, she was my life, my dreams. There was nothing else left, you know?" Jacob paced back and forth waiting, brows furrowed.

"Yes, I believe that it is what you believed, Jacob." The soft, deep voice replied.

Startled, Jacob had nearly forgotten about the man. The large, soft-spoken giant of a man had joined him at the darkest moment of his night. He'd been there at the edge of Jacob's awareness throughout the long, wet watch. Quiet, unobtrusive, he'd waited, never leaving Jacob's side.

"And, there will certainly be much to discuss about the choice you made here, my friend," Rhamiel, the angel sent to retrieve Jacob's soul, continued. "But that's not something to worry about at the moment. Right now we need to think about moving on, Jacob." He rose from where he'd been stooping on one knee next to Jacob.

"We've been here all night, and it's time that we leave," the large man said, placing his hand under Jacob's elbow, urging him to his feet.

"I look so peaceful there, don't I?" Jacob asked. "I mean, it's kind of weird in a way to see my own body lying there like that. I don't hurt, or even feel bad, really. I just couldn't leave it there like that, ya know? With no one knowing where it was? Someone, at least, needed to know where it was...before I...before we...leave." Jacob wished he felt more sure.

After a considering pause, Rhamiel responded, "Yes, I guess you do... look peaceful, that is," placing both his hands behind his back, spreading his feet in a stance like a soldier at ease. "Others will come to take care of your body, Jacob, now that it's been seen. They will make the necessary arrangements."

Studying Jacob's face, he continued, "We've already discussed this. You decided that you don't want to stay for your funeral. Have you changed your mind? Is there something more you'd like to do?"

"No, I just didn't want to leave it here, that's all. You know, with no one knowing," Jacob replied.

"Well, no more waiting," Rhamiel turned and faced him. A bright energy began to thrum as resolute eyes locked firmly onto Jacob's. "It's time, Jacob."

Panic roared in Jacob's ears, gripping his insides. He wanted to run and heave at the same time. His mind raced to find something to say, some way to sidetrack or plead for more time. But he knew there was nothing left he could say, nothing left to do. A sickening awareness that he'd done something irrevocable climbed up Jacob's spine making his neck and shoulders rigid. Regret and fear washed through him. As if he'd known what Jacob had been thinking, Rhamiel spoke.

"There is nothing that cannot be forgiven, Jacob. There's no need to be afraid. Understanding why you chose the solution you did will become your journey now."

Looking into Rhamiel's eyes, Jacob could see the affection the large man had for him. A hint of a smile touched the corners of his mouth, and a curious sense came over Jacob that he knew this man from another time, other journeys. Suddenly, the deep lines that framed the ancient face felt oddly familiar. This strange man who'd patiently sat with him in the cold and dark, through the longest night of his life, was a friend. Rhamiel extended his hand toward Jacob and waited.

Finding courage in the eyes of this newly found old friend, Jacob reached his hand forward, wrapping fingers around the man's forearm in a familiar greeting. Rhamiel returned his grip. Like two soldiers, brothers from many battles fought together, their eyes met in a common understanding, and they were gone.

The sounds of a busy crime scene filled the area surrounding Jacob and Molly's Bridge…now to be known as the location of Canyon Creek's latest broken heart suicide.

CHUCK BAKER

ROAM

Chuck Baker is a retired businessman and widower living in Stroud, OK. Now a published author specializing in human interest short stories, both fact and fiction, many with an ironic ending.

ROAM

by Chuck Baker

After lighting the lantern, Lefty used the pitchfork kept by the door to probe under the bunk beds, behind the potbellied stove, and in the corners where rattlesnakes could be coiled, ready to strike, and finding none, gave the all clear to Memphis Max.

They had left the ranch house after lunch and rode all afternoon to reach the line shack just after dusk. The next three months would be spent rounding up and branding strays, shooting mountain lions, and cutting and storing hay for the winter crew. Montana winters could be cruel, and no fodder for the horses would be more so.

The flickering lantern cast moving shadows throughout the one-room shack as Lefty and Memphis Max rolled out their bedrolls onto the soft feathered mattresses and pulled off their dusty boots to stretch out their tired bodies that had spent half a day in the saddle. Some of the patterns reminded Lefty of the Indian war dances he had seen at a Wild West show five years ago.

The only thing missing was the steady beat of tom-toms, now replaced with the continuous chirp of crickets, but the dancing shadows still looked familiar.

Lefty was a lawyer from Philadelphia who had been caught red-handed bribing a judge for a favorable ruling in a patent infringement suit. The federal prosecutor was so anxious to be rid of him, he had offered Lefty immunity from prosecution with uncontested disbarment in exchange for his testimony and agreement to leave town and state.

The West was opening up, and Lefty heeded Horace Greeley's advice and took a train to St. Louis, where he met a rancher from Montana recruiting cowboys to ride range in big sky country. The pay was low, danger high, and benefits too few to count, but Lefty needed the solitude to reflect on his past, and so he agreed to make the trip to wide open spaces.

Memphis Max was from Memphis, where he worked for his uncle in the foundry. He spent 10 – 12 hours a day shoveling coal into huge blast furnaces to melt iron ore that poured into molds to make farming equipment such as plows, harrows, and iron wheels for freight wagons.

Max had come to St. Louis to attend the wedding of his cousin and met Lefty in the Gilded Garter Saloon.

After a few rounds of barley brew, Lefty convinced Max the fresh air, wide-open spaces, and freedom from family was a solid decision and convinced him to join Mr. Corbin on a Western quest.

They had worked for Mr. Corbin on the Lonely C Ranch for seven years and spent the past three years at the ranch having no contact with the outside world, in order to save their money for a joint business venture, and this would be their last stint at the line shack. When their three-month tour was over, they would tell Mr. Corbin *adios* and step in their own direction.

As Memphis Max was starting a fire in the potbellied stove, Lefty took the lantern hanging outside to the babbling brook behind the shack to get a bucket of water for coffee. The crackling of the fire was the only noise in the shack as Lefty and Max sipped steamy coffee from metal cups and listened to the lonely howl of a pair of coyotes greeting the full moon rising in the east.

"What are we going to do with the money we saved?" Lefty asked, when the howls finally ceased.

"I've been thinking, with these wide-open spaces and all these cattle, we should make some sort of wire fence that would keep the cattle in one place. We wouldn't have to ride range and round up strays. Be no reason for line shacks, and nobody's herds would get mixed in, so there would be no reason for trouble to start," replied Max.

"That sounds like a good idea," chimed Lefty, as he refreshed their cups and added, "what would you call it?"

"I don't know, maybe wonder wire," was Max's response.

Lefty blew the steam from his cup and asked, "How would we do it?"

Max had been thinking about this since his first trip to a line shack many years ago, and he bubbled over as he explained to Lefty. "We buy spools of wire from my uncle and a cable twisting machine that will stick a six-inch piece of wire between two wires twisted together about every six inches, and those sharp points will stick the cows if they lean against it, so they won't push through it."

Over the next three months, Lefty and Max spent every waking hour making plans, drawing schematics for the patent office, estimating costs, and outlining sales and marketing strategy, as they went about their chores.

Three days before the relief crew was due, Max put away supper dishes, poured coffee in their metal cups, and joined Lefty sitting by the white-barked aspen growing on the banks of the brook. Lefty had seemed reserved the last few days, causing Max to doubt his commitment to their project.

As he handed Lefty his coffee and seated himself against the tree trunk, he asked, with a worried tone, "Lefty, are you sure you want to be my business partner?"

Lefty, staring at the snowcapped mountain on the horizon, let his eyes follow a hawk lazily circling above the field below and carefully considered how to answer his good friend. "Max, I agreed to be your partner, because you need someone to help you. I'll keep books and manage inventory and distribution, while you keep the plant running.

You need someone to do that, and your choices are me, or hire someone you don't know to do it for you, and that could lead to disaster, so I agreed to be your partner."

Max listened intently and followed up, "I appreciate that, but do you really want to be my partner?"

Lefty focused his gaze on Max's furrowed brow and answered, "I told you I would be your partner."

With a hint of aggravation in his tone, Max shot back, "I heard what you said. Let's talk about what you want to do."

Lefty's eyes returned to the mountain range as he rolled Max's question over in his mind and took a sip of coffee before responding to the inquiry. "I feel responsible for you being here. When Mr. Corbin described Montana, I could almost taste the freedom. When I met you, it seemed you needed freedom too, so I talked you into coming with me. With our freedom comes responsibility, and helping you is the responsible thing to do."

Max wasn't going to let Lefty off so lightly and pursued, "I get that, what would you really like to do?"

Lefty swatted at a horsefly buzzing around with his hand, then said almost wistfully, "If I could do what I want to do, I would roam around these United States and look at the cost of freedom.

"Old Abe said about the proclamation of emancipation 'in giving freedom to the slave, we assure freedom to the free.' He engaged in war to assure that freedom, and I would like to roam around and enjoy it now that the war is over."

Max pondered long and hard on Lefty's answer before quizzing, "Would you rather do that or go in business with me?"

Without hesitation, Lefty answered, "When I was fourteen years old, my grandmother asked me to go to church with her one Sunday, and the preacher was reading out of the *Bible*, and he said, 'Where the Spirit of the Lord is, there is liberty'. From that day since, I have yearned to be free. If I wasn't committed to being a partner with you, I would roam around looking for the Spirit of the Lord, so I would be assured of that liberty if I found it, but you and I are partners until you say no."

Max chewed on that like a termite on wood rot and finally said, "Lefty, you're the only friend I have, and I wouldn't do anything to stop you from doing what you want to do.

"I'm honored you think we can do this, but if you were not to be my partner, I'd go to California. I got a letter from my brother out in Colomo at Sutters Mill, and he said gold nuggets flow down the mountain streams, fruit and vegetables grow as big as a mare's hoof, and the weather is always comfortable. I could live like that.

Now, I told you what I would do. Tell me what you would do if we weren't partners."

Lefty returned his gaze to the majestic mountains, tossed the cold coffee from the tin cup into the brook and said almost to himself, "When I look at those mountains, sometimes I see myself riding through them, and I reach a plateau. I stop to rest my horse and look back to see where I've been; then I turn around and look ahead to see where I'm going. If we weren't partners, I would go look for that plateau."

Satisfied Lefty wasn't holding anything back, Max stuck out his hand and said, "Then let's shake on it."

Lefty reached out with a firm grip and a hearty shake as they both agreed, "It's a deal."

The seven hour ride back to the ranch house was quiet, as they had spent three months planning, and now both were occupied with sorting through what each one had to do. They decided to wait until morning to ask Mr. Corbin for their pay and tell him they were leaving.

The ranch was a two-day ride from a little mining camp called Billings where they stabled their horses, ate a steak, and got rooms at the hotel, as the camp had become a town.

The next morning, after a hearty breakfast of ham steak as big as a saddle blanket and three eggs staring at them with fried turnips at the hotel dining room, they made their way to the post office to mail their patent application and orders for equipment.

Before getting to the post office, they passed the hardware store and had to step off the sidewalk because of the rolls of wire stacked in front of the store. Leaning against the rolls was a homemade sign that read "Barbed Wire: $2 a Roll".

Max instantly recognized his invention and scurried inside to talk to the proprietor.

Upon learning that a peddler from Illinois had passed through last year and sold him a distributorship, Max looked at Lefty and said, "That ends our deal; let's go have a drink."

At the Broken Branch Saloon, they said their good-byes, and Max asked, "By the way, you're right handed. Why do they call you Lefty?"

The slight curl of a smile crossed his lips as he snickered, "Because I left Pennsylvania." After an uproarious belly laugh and a hard leg slap, Max added, "One more thing: which way are you heading?"

Lefty took a long pull on his whiskey glass, looked through the swinging doors, and said softly, "It doesn't matter; all roads lead to roam."

ALICIA BALLARD

SILVER DOLLAR EYES

Alicia Ballard is a student at Redlands Community College in El Reno, Oklahoma and an employee of the El Reno Carnegie Library. She actually was a member of our writing group before she joined the library staff! Alicia is also a gifted horror writer.

SILVER DOLLAR EYES

by Alicia Ballard

The woman in the white hat walks alone in the woods. Many have seen her; fewer have spoken to her. I am not one of those few. They say her name is Virginia, Virginia Tsukiko. They also say she drowned her children in the lake down the dirt road in the woods.

Some say she's not really there, that she strung herself up shortly after her kids were gone. I've seen her, Virginia in her white hat, carrying a dripping bundle. Sometimes she looks back while I follow behind her. Silver dollars over her eyes, her smile is so sad it breaks my heart.

Some say they can hear her, crying for her children, crying for forgiveness. I have yet to hear her cries. They say her cries can drive a person mad. They say a lot of things about her, but I say they do not know her. I know her, that poor Virginia in her pretty white hat. So accursed, so sad.

Maybe she'll come for me, for what I did, for what the townspeople say she did. For now, she just looks back on me, silver dollar eyes shining, and she smiles her sad knowing smile back on her husband, her husband that took his three little ones to the lake. She tried to stop me. She hit me and bit me, but in the end, I succeeded. Poor Virginia, in her pretty white hat, the hat I bought for her when our eldest was born.

Now I hear her; she's calling my name. Sometimes it sounds just like the wind, but I know it's her. She's coming for me at last, and I'm ready. I feel her cold hands creep up my chest, her long icy fingers wrap around my throat. She comes into view now, blonde hair visible beneath the brim of her pretty white hat, silver dollar eyes glinting in the moonlight. Her smile has changed; it's no longer sad, no longer knowing. It stretches from ear to ear, small sharp teeth shining. Revenge has come at last. As my vision darkens, I see my children, blue skinned. I cannot hear what they are saying, yet their mouths move. They smile, small white teeth and silver dollar eyes glinting in tune with their mother's.

The sweet hand of death takes me as their faces finally give in to darkness. Goodbye, Virginia, with her pretty white hat. Goodbye, Children, with your blue faces. Goodbye, wooded road with your lake placed peacefully to one side. It's time for me to receive my own silver dollar eyes.

JUDY BISHOP

NEW FRONTIERS

Judy K. Bishop writes inspirational children's books, poetry, short stories and essays. Before becoming involved in the greater Oklahoma City writing scene, she previously lived in Hawaii for almost twenty years. She currently resides in Choctaw, OK.

NEW FRONTIERS

by Judy Bishop

The room was small, dingy and musty smelling. Lizzie was scared and alone, with no family nor anyone else who cared. This must be a dream; it couldn't possibly be real. Yet somewhere inside, she knew her situation was her reality, even though she was trying to pretend otherwise. She sat staring at the iron bars in her cell that kept her captive.

Tomorrow would be the last day of her life. Lizzie would meet her fate in the morning and be the first woman in the Nevada Territory, or any territory for that matter, to be hanged.

She kept fighting the fear, trying to keep it from escalating. In the cell next to her were two drunken outlaws, and they kept taunting her and making crude remarks. How had her life come to this? She had come to Nevada with her Uncle Lester as a twelve-year-old child and lived a somewhat happy life for the next eight years until he died three years ago.

Looking around, Lizzie knew there was no hope.

The fact that she was innocent had not saved her. Convicted at her trial, she knew the judge had no option but to follow the law and pass down her sentence of death by hanging—a life cut way too short and full of tragedy and hardship. There had been plenty of time in this cramped unbearable place to think back on her life and how she ended up in this situation.

At nine years of age, Lizzie was orphaned when her parents died from an unknown illness. She had no living relatives except Uncle Lester who was her mother's brother and who had never married nor had any children. He was reluctant to take on the role of raising Lizzie after her parents passed, as he could barely take care of himself.

Uncle Lester was a dreamer and a drunk. He had always been the black sheep of his family. Now, here was this child who needed him, and he would either decide to become her guardian or she would be sent to an orphanage. He wasn't particularly fond of children as a whole and knew nothing about raising them, especially a girl.

Lizzie was spunky and, at times, very stubborn. She would be a handful as she got older. Uncle Lester weighed the pros and cons of the situation. Not many pros, except one major one.

Lizzie's parents had been somewhat wealthy, and she would inherit everything since she had no other siblings.

The dreamer in Lester could think of a lot of good uses for all that money. His weakness for the whiskey bottle had always gotten him into trouble and ruined any good that came into his life. Here would be a chance to start over and open up a whole new world for him.

Finally, greed, more than family obligation, got the best of him, and he decided to take on the responsibility of raising his niece. So it began, the child and the drunken uncle starting a new life together.

It was rough going for a couple of years, with Lizzie used to being spoiled by her rich parents and Uncle Lester used to losing himself in the bottle and being accountable to no one. It was a big adjustment for them both. The drunken binges were even more frequent now that he had more money.

Lizzie often was home alone for days at a time while Uncle Lester was out on his drinking binges. Having to get herself up and ready for school most of the time, she began to lose interest and began skipping school frequently.

School authorities took notice and began questioning Lizzie about her home life and frequent absences from school. Uncle Lester came to the realization he could have Lizzie taken away from him, and with her would go the money. Something had to change.

It was 1863. News of gold and silver strikes in Nevada, Wyoming and California, as well as other states, were swirling around daily. People were leaving in droves to claim free land the government had made available or to try their hands at prospecting for gold or silver.

Opportunities abounded in this new frontier, and the dreamer in Uncle Lester was reawakened. Things were getting worse with Lizzie, and besides, when she turned twenty-one, she would have control of her money, be on her own, and he would no longer be her guardian. This new venture sounded like a great opportunity for Uncle Lester.

A decision made, Uncle Lester and Lizzie headed West to a new beginning and a new dream. He would lay claim to some land in Nevada, strike it rich with silver or gold, then live out the rest of his life with no worries.

Early spring of 1864, Uncle Lester and Lizzie left St. Louis and headed west to start a new life.

Lizzie never looked back, as she hated school and St. Louis with its reminders of her parents and the wonderful life she once had with them.

Joining a wagon train headed for Nevada, they were among twenty wagons of families like them who had hopes and dreams of new beginnings and better lives.

None of the families, including Lizzie and Uncle Lester, could have been prepared for the brutal trip ahead of them, with hardships beyond imagination. Spring floods took their toll, and some of the homesteaders were lost trying to cross a flooded river. Babies were born, people died from sickness, and each day was long and grueling. Not easy for a young girl and a man who had never done a hard day of labor in his life. Always looming in everyone's mind was the threat of Indian attacks or thefts, buffalo herds, storms and broken wagon wheels.

Lizzie and Uncle Lester survived the four month ordeal, arriving in Nevada anxious to start their new lives. He would be prospecting, instead of farming, so he decided not to lay claim to any homestead land, but instead purchased a small house on the edge of town where Lizzie would be safer while he was away prospecting.

Three years passed with Uncle Lester away much of the time, looking for that "miracle strike," but times were good when he was home with Lizzie.

Lizzie was doing well in her new life. She reluctantly attended school regularly, and being a bit on the spunky and wild side, mingled more with the boys who were more daring and fun. The girls were soft and boring, constantly giggling and chasing after the boys.

She was not interested in anything more than a friendship with any boy. However, the boys felt differently about Lizzie. Her long black hair, striking green eyes and lean tall body gave her an exciting, somewhat wild look, as she always let her long hair hang loose past her shoulders, not braided or pinned up like the other girls.

Then it happened, the "miracle strike" Uncle Lester had been dreaming about since the day they arrived in Nevada. It was a modest strike, but enough that he could quit prospecting and live off this new-found wealth for many years to come. He even cut down on his drinking and spent more time with Lizzie. She and Uncle Lester grew close, and she loved him dearly. He felt the same about her; she was the light of his life.

Life was good for five years until the day Uncle Lester, pushing his luck too far, was shot and killed in a dispute during a poker game. Lizzie was twenty years old and truly on her own now. Uncle Lester had gambled away most of Lizzie's money and his own small fortune. She wasn't sure what to do but was thankful Uncle Lester had purchased the house they lived in upon their arrival in Nevada, so at least she had a roof over her head.

She began hanging around outside the saloon waiting for men who had too much to drink to stagger outside, where she would smile and tease them with her beauty and manage to get some money from them for her time.

There was a brothel down the street from the saloon, and Lizzie began to take notice of the women there dressed in fancy clothes and making a good living off the miners who came to town. The madam of the brothel took note of Lizzie and offered her a job. She was younger than the other women and very popular with the men.

Things went along well for a couple years until a young cowboy named Sonny came to town with a cattle herd they were moving south to the railroad line in order to ship to the stockyards in Colorado.

Sonny took a real fancy to Lizzie, and she became his favorite. Being out on the trail for months put a real thirst in a man for a good-looking woman. Lizzie certainly was that, with her long black hair and feisty attitude. Sonny wasn't especially good looking but was free with his money, so Lizzie put up with a lot from him, even though he would get rough at times and occasionally slap her around.

Then came the time he went too far. Sonny had come into the brothel, so drunk he could hardly walk and, of course, wanted Lizzie.

More rough than usual, he knocked her against the wall. She fell to the floor, hitting her head and was dazed. Sonny came after her again, grabbing her arm to pull her up, intending to give her more of the same.

It was then, Lizzie, lightheaded and fed up with the roughness, grabbed Sonny's gun from his holster and told him to let her go. He stepped back, laughed, then lunged at her to take the gun away. There was a loud ear-piercing noise as the gun fired, and Sonny dropped to the floor.

People came into the room as Sonny lay dying on the floor, uttering his last words as he pointed to Lizzie. "She was trying to rob me, and then shot me."

Lizzie stood there in disbelief and panic. "It was an accident; he was beating me. It was self-defense."

It was only a matter of minutes before Sheriff Stone rushed in to find Lizzie standing over the dead man and a crowd gathering. There were no witnesses to the abuse from Sonny, only witnesses to his statement that she shot him while trying to rob him. Therefore, he had to take Lizzie to jail.

Now here she sat in her cell, one day away from the hangman's noose. A rushed trial had come about with the town women influencing the men on the jury and ending with her being convicted. Some of their husbands had been with Lizzie, and they aimed to get rid of her and make her pay.

The next morning, the sun rose shining brightly through Lizzie's small cell window. Here she was, her last day of life. Lizzie was very scared but tried to will her body to stop shaking. A crowd had gathered behind the jail where the hanging would take place. She could hear the excitement and anticipation rising in their voices.

The jailhouse door opened. Sheriff Stone came in and walked up to Lizzie's cell.

"Sorry Lizzie, time to go."

He regretted the situation, but his hands were tied. There had been a legal trial and sentence handed down by the judge. As she walked outside, she could see the smirks on the women's faces and the guilt and sadness on the men's. It just didn't seem right to hang a woman, no matter what she had done.

She walked up the steps to the gallows where Sheriff Stone then tied her hands behind her back. The rope was tight and cut into her wrists. Lizzie's breathing became more labored, and she had trouble swallowing. Trying to calm herself, she took a deep breath, not wanting the crowd to see the terror she was starting to feel. Sheriff Stone asked if she had any last words.

Lizzie shook her head from side to side. What was there to say? This was the end. There would be no daring cowboy riding into town, his horse at full speed, rescuing her and then riding off into the unknown together to live happily ever after. She was about to face her fate; nothing she could say would change that.

The hangman put a hood over her head and stepped away. Silence was all around as the crowd waited, and Lizzie's breathing became even more labored.

She closed her eyes and thought of her beautiful childhood in St. Louis with her parents and her life here in Nevada with her beloved Uncle Lester. Oh, how she wished her life could have played out in happiness and her dreams fulfilled. Her mind wandered off into the fairytale of what might have been.

Then came the sound of creaking wood piercing the silence as the hangman pulled the lever that dropped the platform out from under her feet. There was a gasp from the crowd . . . then chilling silence.

GLENDA BROWN

STAGECOACH TO NOWHERE

Glenda Brown is a writer with a wry sense of humor that shows in her short stories. She is a former social worker who lives with her husband Dan in Yukon, Ok. She is currently writing a mystery.

STAGECOACH TO NOWHERE

by Glenda Brown

Walterine Hoog stood at the edge of Main Street anxiously awaiting the arrival of The Butterfield Overland Stage. The man who sold her the ticket told her the stage is usually late. He told her not to worry. There could be a number of reasons why the stage was not on time. She was not worried about the stage being late, she was overwhelmed to make such a trip alone, and almost penniless.

The morning heat was already stifling in the small town of El Paso, Texas. The year was 1860, and El Paso was yet to become a boomtown. The railroad had yet to arrive along with the saloons, prostitutes, and gambling houses which would create a thriving economy for some. They would line Main Street in a fury of lifestyle that the town of El Paso had never known. Until the boomtown arrived, there was literally no opportunity for a young woman to find employment.

She wiped sweat from her beautiful face with a white handkerchief and tried to be patient like the ticket man told her to be. She stood beside one suitcase.

It contained all her earthy possessions which consisted of two dresses, a pair of what she called her Sunday shoes, needles, thread, and a few pieces of jewelry that her mother swore were valuable. Pinned inside the thick layers of white petticoat with two safety pins was $50.00 which was all she had left after buying her ticket to San Francisco. This small amount of money included the sale of the farm along with the horses, cows, chickens and all the farm equipment.

A few weeks after her parents died suddenly from a fever, Mr. Nixon, the banker in town, came to see her and offered to buy the property. Mr. Nixon was a short bald man with the bushiest eyebrows she had ever seen. It made him look as if his hair had fallen from the top of his head and landed right above his eyes. He peeked from under his heavy brows with small beady eyes. His shyster looks gave him the appearance of being a pettifogger.

Walterine did not know about her father's indebtedness to the bank until Mr. Nixon bluntly informed her of this pending obligation.

After the debt was paid in full, Walterine barely had enough money for her fare. She was told the cost of her ticket included meals and lodging at the way stations.

With such a small amount of money to make a long trip like this, she would need to watch every penny.

She packed only what she thought she could manage. Mr. Nixon, seeing how distraught she was, offered to store her belongings at no cost, until she could make other arrangements. She thanked him for his thoughtfulness but declined. It was pure anguish to know that she would soon be departing from the only world she had ever known.

The tightness in her chest made her feel as if she could hardly breathe. Only with divine help could she possibly carry on. There would be no reason to return to El Paso. She had no family or anyone in town that she could count on. She was paralyzed with fear of what lay ahead. Trying to think clearly of what was best for her, she came to the conclusion that she would buy a ticket to San Francisco. At least she'd heard stories about the place. She remembered when she was a young girl. Her mother told her tales about how exciting it was to live in a big city, a place where people were coming and going constantly and always had plenty to do.

She told her about the dress shops where clothes were bought, ready to wear, the fancy restaurants where people dressed in their Sunday best to dine, of the theatres and all the places people went to indulge and show others their prosperity. Just the name "San Francisco" sounded magical.

Walterine knew her mother had never been to San Francisco. It was a made-up story by a lonely woman who wanted to put a spark of hope in her young daughter's life. She knew her mother never had a store-bought dress to wear or any special party to attend. Her life had been filled with hard work and loneliness. Her mother knew only the sounds of prairie where coyotes howled after dark, and the wind moaned night and day without stopping.

At times, she had wanted to scream at her mother, "Please stop with the lies!" but she did not have the heart to tell her mother that she knew it was all untrue and that the places she was talking about were all make believe. Now, she was acting like her mother, dreaming and making plans that weren't real. One thing about dreams, they always hang out there in the darkness, almost within reach.

Now, it was time to face reality. The moment had come. She was on her way to a city of make-believe. She fought back tears of dread. When life seemed unbearable, she would think of God and of his benevolent guidance. Our Lord had promised never to leave or forsake us if we obeyed Him. If ever she needed God, it was now. She believed the Spirit was telling her "San Francisco".

She needed time to think and carry out her plans. With San Francisco being so far away, it gave her time to make the right decision. At last, the stage appeared. She had seen stagecoaches before when she accompanied her parents to town to buy supplies. She never paid much attention to them before. Now, this would be her home for the next two weeks or more.

Taking a closer look at the coach, she noticed a graceful swinging motion of the carriage instead of jolting up and down. This would be a good thing. She had been concerned about the rough ride and wondered how she would manage it. She heard stories of the hardships of travels, the danger of being robbed or killed by outlaws, along with almost intolerable travel conditions. But this was her only option to travel.

Standing in the stifling heat, she observed the coach was painted a dark blue with a bright yellow undercarriage. The window in the door was glazed. The side windows were not. There was canvas covering above each window which could be rolled up or down depending on the weather. The interior was much nicer than she expected. There were three upholstered benches which looked like they could accommodate maybe a dozen people.

The driver quickly jumped down. He picked up her suitcase as if it were weightless and threw it haphazardly on top of the coach. It landed with such a bang that a passenger already seated inside the stage began to complain.

"You would think they would treat our belongings with some respect," she mumbled. "My dear, I hope you didn't have anything breakable."

As Walterine stepped inside the coach, she assured the complaining lady that she did not. Before she could get herself seated comfortably, the stage was on its way.

"Where are you going?" a very pretty lady in a green satin dress with a hat to match asked her.

Walterine thought her to be the most beautiful woman she had ever seen. Her clothing was exquisite. The lady seated next to her was dressed equally as beautiful. They both looked her up and down, like she was the likes they had never seen before.

"I'm going to San Francisco," Walterine said in a very timid voice. Before she started the trip, she felt that her clothing was adequate, but now she did not.

"My dear, do you have any idea how long this trip is going to be? You are traveling so lightly."

Walterine did not have the heart to tell them that all she owned in the world was packed in one small suitcase. She felt close to tears and felt that she might break down when suddenly the young man across from her asked a question.

"Do you have family in San Francisco?" His voice did not have the prying tone of the two snobby women. He was dressed in a tailored suit with a glistening white shirt. His shoes were very polished and looked expensive. He was strikingly handsome. He laid his newspaper down on his lap and introduced himself as Durston Fort. He tipped his hat and told her that he was very pleased to meet her.

Walterine knew that the young man was trying to rescue her from the two meddling women. She wanted to show her gratitude for this act of kindness. Walterine tried to answer his question politely even though she knew it was a big lie.

"I have an aunt who lives there. She owns a hat shop, and I am going there to work for her."

Both women looked at each other as if they doubted her story. Walterine prayed that no one would ask her any more questions about the shop. She felt her story did not sound very credible, and she wished they would stop with the questions.

The young handsome man buried himself again behind his newspaper with the feeling that he had successfully interrupted the interrogation of the shabby girl who seemed so intimidated by the two women. He doubted it would last very long.

The second man that sat beside Durston Fort was a Mr. Horace Mills. He introduced himself to Walterine but did not give any information about himself. She was grateful for this. Walterine thought him dull-looking and very unattractive. She imagined him to be some sort of businessman on his way to some big important meeting.

The third man was the least desirable of all. He was heavy-set with a beard that looked in need of a trim. His name was Teed Riley. His face had a long scar down his left cheek. He looked like a fighter who had no fear. He was no doubt a tough man. He wore a gun on his hip, and he looked mean enough to use it for whatever reason he had.

They traveled about two more hours when Durston smiled at her the second time during the trip. She smiled back. It would be nice to have a pleasant conversation with someone so nice.

"You're a long way from home," he said. "If I can be of any assistance, let me know." He said it like he really meant it.

"Is your family from San Francisco?" Mrs. Dunn spoke up again, not caring that this question had already been asked.

"No," Walterine answered back quickly, "just my aunt." She did not want to talk any more about a town she knew nothing about.

"Most of my family is from…" then her mind went blank. She could not think straight. She did not like to lie. In all her young years, she didn't find any predicament that needed made-up stories.

Since she had started this trip, it seemed that all she was doing was making up lies to keep from embarrassing herself. Guilt rushed over her as she sat there, trying to fabricate more believable stories.

"Well," she stammered. "I've been away a long time, and I hardly remember anything or anyone."

Now she had the attention of everyone, especially Teed Riley. A young beautiful girl traveling alone and not completely sure where she came from or where she was going?

The man named Teed spoke up. "Well, girl, are you from the North, South, East or West?" He spoke very loudly as he took his cigar from between his rubbery lips. They all looked at her…waiting for an answer, except Durston. Why couldn't they mind their own business? She was not hammering them with questions.

Walterine felt put upon. Maybe her lies would catch up with her sooner than later. She could not let these prying people get the best of her. Just because she looked penniless did not give them the right to badger her. She knew she was stuck with them for the time being, so she tried to appease them with an answer.

"I'm originally from the North," she said, not looking at anyone in particular.

"The North," Teed bellowed. "You don't sound like you're from up North. You sound more like you are from Kansas, like a farm girl." Walterine had no idea which direction was Kansas. She didn't know much about any place other than El Paso.

"We are waiting, girl," Teed said very sarcastically.

"Well, I am really from the North South," she stammered, hoping this would satisfy their curiosity.
She heard a few sighs, then chuckles.

"I think something is wrong," Mrs. Dunn whispered under her breath to Mrs. Atkinson.

Everyone got quiet. The conversation came to a complete stop. Walterine continued to look down at her clenched hands.

Durston sat quietly behind his paper. She hoped he would come to her rescue again; this time he did not.

Travel was quiet for the next few hours. The stage had stopped several times for the passengers to relieve themselves. The three women went in one direction, and the men went in the opposite. The stop was short.

Soon they were on their way again. The next stop of any duration was a way station. Walterine was starved, and her bones ached from being cramped. They had traveled for what seemed like eternity when the driver announced they would be stopping for the night.

Accommodations would be few, but it would be a chance to get a warm meal, a sponge bath and a bed for the night. Walterine was disappointed when the man who managed the way station brought out a big pot of beans, along with a pan of corn bread. He placed bowls and spoons on the table and told everyone to help themselves.

She could see steam coming from the pot of beans. They looked delicious. She was the first to dip from the large pot. She filled her bowl half full and then took a piece of bread. She took a large bite of cornbread and found it to be completely tasteless, like cornmeal and water. She then tried the beans. They were no better.

She noticed the look on the other two women's faces as they frowned and forced themselves to eat. Everyone knew it would be hours before anything was available again.

Bedroom accommodations were not any better.

She shared a room with the two other women who snored most of the night. Walterine slept little and was glad to see the morning come. Mrs. Atkinson arose and started complaining immediately about not getting any sleep. Both women were inquisitive about Walterine sleeping in her dress.

After a quick breakfast of fried eggs and sausage, the party was on its way again. The road seemed endless. It was sticky hot during the day with everyone's clothes glued to their wet, perspiring bodies.

The evenings were somewhat cooler, but the mosquitoes made life miserable after dark. The days came and went uneventfully. Travel was pure hell.

They had been traveling for four more days when she heard Durston talking favorably about the next town they were approaching. The town had hotels, restaurants, and a general store. There were several saloons for the men to indulge in much needed drinks. They would be spending the night.

Mrs. Atkinson offered to share a hotel room with Walterine to cut down on expenses, but Walterine refused. She could not tolerate her constant meddling. Even if she had to pay with her last penny, she wanted some peace and quiet.

The entrance to the hotel was very lovely. Walterine had never seen such fine furnishings. A white settee with lilac pillows faced the doorway. There were vases of fresh flowers on a long table that sat by the window. A scent of lavender was in the air. Walterine breathed in the luscious fragrance, wanting to remain in the lobby forever. She took her room key and made her way to the top of the stairs.

The key said Room 15. She found her room to be more than suitable, with a big bed which was very soft with two large pillows.

She sank into the softness of the bed and was asleep as soon as her head hit the pillow. She slept fitfully for about five hours. When she awoke, she realized that she had missed dinner with the other two ladies. If they had knocked on her door, she had not heard them.

Her window faced the street and she could hear people talking below. As she looked out, she saw only darkness. She looked at the clock. It was 11 o'clock. She was now wide awake and hungry. She wondered if any restaurants were still open, but she doubted it.

She straightened her dress and combed her hair. She didn't like the idea of being alone on the street. It was not safe. She took the large hatpin out of her suitcase and placed it in a pocket for protection. She could do a lot of damage to anyone who tried to harm her. She closed the door very gently behind her, so she would not make any noise. She tiptoed down the stairs, being very careful not to disturb anyone. She felt like she was doing something sinister tiptoeing so gingerly.

When she got to the street, she picked up her pace. She walked down the sidewalk until she came to a saloon. She was starving and very thirsty. Maybe she could get a sandwich or something to eat.

The noise was loud, and everyone inside seemed to be having a great time. She knew that respectable women didn't dare set foot in such places, but she was too hungry to care.

She had never been in a saloon before, and this one time couldn't be all that bad. She was not planning on making it a habit...What would it hurt if she paid a short visit to see what was going on and maybe get a morsel of food? As she walked inside, she prayed that no one would recognize her.

She looked around the saloon for any men traveling companions. She did not see them. It was late, and they had probably retired for the night. Two saloon girls were looking at her very mysteriously. They whispered for a moment; then the girl with curly blonde hair approached her.

"Do you want something, honey?" she asked sarcastically.

"Yes," Walterine answered. "I will have a cold beer." Walterine realized how out of place she looked in her gingham girlish attire.

The saloon girl smiled. She swung her hips wildly as she made her way back to the bartender to get the drink. She came back and set the glass on the table in front of Walterine.

"The manager says, 'it's on the house.'" She gave Walterine another smile, then walked away. Walterine lifted the glass of liquid to her mouth. She took a little sip. It was cold and refreshing. She expected it to be bitter. The taste was sweet, and she really liked it. If beer tasted like this, maybe more women should try it. She downed the sweet tasting liquid in a few seconds. She saw the saloon girl approaching her table again.

"I'll have another beer." She licked her lips as she spoke.

"Oh, really?" the saloon girl said, grinning from ear to ear. "You sure you want beer or another glass of cold apple cider?"

Walterine could feel her cheeks reddening. She'd made a fool of herself again. She picked up her purse and made her way out the door. The streets were now completely empty and dark.

A very skinny old man was sweeping the doorway in front of the bar.

"We're closing," he said. "You need to get yourself home, young lady."

Suddenly, Walterine felt scared. She didn't have far to go to get back to her hotel room, but she didn't like walking even a short distance. She was alone on the streets in a strange town, and she knew no one. She questioned herself, why had she ventured from her room in the middle of the night? She scolded herself as she walked quickly down the dark streets.

Suddenly, a shadow appeared in the alley, and before she could muster a scream, large hairy hands were around her throat, cutting off her air.

She realized she would die if she didn't do something. She remembered the hatpin she had in her pocket for protection. With one free hand, she reached deep into her pocket and pulled out the pin. She swung it with all her might at the hairy arms that held her captive. As she plunged the pin deep into one of his hands, he let go.

He wheeled around and stood facing her. He looked down at her with the eyes of a madman. Still holding the hatpin, she plunged it into his chest. He clutched his chest as he fell at her feet. Blood sprayed her face and dress.

She had never been so scared in her life. All she could think of was to flee. She looked down at the blood that covered her dress.

Realizing she was still holding the hatpin, she placed it back into her pocket. She was shaking violently and trying to regain her composure. She tried to take a step, then discovered she had lost a shoe in the struggle. She reached down to pick up the shoe, when she noticed something lying on the ground. The gaslight from the street cast a soft stream of light across the front of the alley way.

She looked again and realized it was a large roll of money. She looked both ways; then she stooped down and grabbed up the money. She put it in her pocket with the hatpin. She broke into a run back to the hotel.

When she entered, the lobby was all quiet. The man at the desk was fast asleep and in the same position she had seen him earlier when she had left the hotel. She made her way up the stairs until she came to Room 15. She unlocked the door and collapsed into the room. She was holding her breath to keep from crying out loud. It was so good to be behind locked doors.

She sat silently for a few minutes, then she pulled the roll of money from her pocket. She had never in her life seen so much money. There were hundreds of dollars, so much that she was too tired to count it.

She removed her blood-soaked dress and hid it along with the money at the bottom of her suitcase. She was just too tired to think. She put on a clean dress and went straight to bed.

Morning came too early. She washed her face and combed her long black hair. She was ready in no time to join Mrs. Atkinson and the other lady downstairs for a quick breakfast of bacon and eggs. She barely had time to swallow the last bite when they announced the stage was leaving.

Walterine was the last one to board. The others had reclaimed their seats and were settled in for the long hot journey ahead of them.

The stage was pulling out of town when Durston said, "Did you hear about the First National Bank being robbed last night? Rumor is there were two men. One got away, but they found a dead man in the alley this morning. They think he is one of the bank robbers, because he fit the description. No gunshots in him, just a large puncture wound in his chest. They figure that's how he died. Another strange thing is, the sheriff didn't find any money on him. So it looks like one of them got away with the bank money. I think the key to the whole mystery is the dead man in the alley."

Durston folded his newspaper back into his lap. "When they find out who he is, the sheriff will have something to go on."

"I agree with you," said Mr. Mills, as he crossed his short legs trying to make himself more comfortable.

"I feel the same way," Teed Riley spoke up.

"With all that money taken from the bank, I am sure they will be offering a big reward. I think all of us should try to remember anything out of the usual last night."

The large man with the smelly cigar was now grinning at Walterine. Walterine felt her body going limp. What would she do? She felt they were saying those things directly to her. Were they picking up her demeanor? Could they see that she seemed nervous when they talked about the murder? She clenched her fists as the stage traveled its slow pace. Would this trip ever end?

It seemed like they had traveled a thousand more dreary miles. She was near tears when she heard the driver announce they were coming into Yuma. Hope welled up in her. She would get off the stage. She would tell the driver that she was sick and needed some time to rest. She felt she did not need to explain to anyone else. She needed to rid herself of their eyes.

The stage pulled on to Main Street and stopped. Durston and the other two men got off first. Everyone seemed in a hurry to stretch his or her legs. The two ladies were headed to a restaurant for coffee, the men to the nearest saloon. Walterine found one of the drivers and asked that he retrieve her suitcase.

She gave him a fast explanation that she would not be going on with them.

He seemed exhausted and did not care. He did not ask her any questions, just handed her the small suitcase. Walterine walked slowly away from the stage, her mind racing. Was she doing the right thing? Should she go back and tell the sheriff what really happened? That she was only defending herself? Would anyone believe her at this point? Why had she run away?

All of a sudden, the suitcase felt so heavy in her small hands. She wasn't sure of anything now. Was she crazy to think that God had dropped all this money at her feet? How could she be sure?

As she crossed the street, she saw a ragged little girl standing in front of a hotel. Was this some kind of omen from heaven? Her heart began to race. She shifted the suitcase from one hand to the other.

She stopped for a minute to look at her surroundings. She liked what she saw. She had a lot of thinking to do, and she was convinced that she had chosen the right place.

ALTON "TUNA" DOBBINS

RAILROADING

Alton "Tuna" Dobbins retired from the Air Force in 1996 with over 2000 hours in single seat attack jets. He then worked for the Federal Aviation Administration as a technical writer until retiring in 2015. Tuna is the author of two fiction novels published by Tate Publishing: *Crossbow Revenge* and *Alice Was Not Her Name,* both action-packed murder mysteries. *Crossbow Revenge* was released early in 2016. *Alice Was Not Her Name* is expected to be released late 2016 or early 2017. Tuna is a fan of fast cars and participates in shows and open road racing in his Corvette. He resides in Mustang, OK with his wife Susan.

RAILROADING

by Alton "Tuna" Dobbins

November 1883, the Atchison, Topeka and Santa Fe Railroad had switched to "standard" time, meaning that almost all depots and stations in Kansas were now on the same "Central Standard Time Zone" clock. A few far western counties in Kansas decided to go with "Mountain Standard Time" so they could stay associated with Colorado. Before switching, ATSF used three different time zones just for Kansas, and that was becoming a hassle. Nearly all United States railroads switched to "standard" time that month on the eighteenth. Some railroads switched last month, and there were a few holdouts not wanting to step into the future, but none of those ran in Kansas.

Most cities and towns still used local time, based on high noon in the middle of the town. Getting the town folk to switch over to "standard" time would take a little longer. The dispatcher and ticket office at the train station in Dodge City had been telling everyone to show up thirty to forty-five minutes early so they wouldn't miss the train.

All the engineers, firemen, brakemen and conductors were required to have their watches set to "standard" time, so there wouldn't be any problems. Everyone else working for the railroad or associated with railroad operations was switching to "standard" time, also. Dodge City was in the western part of the Central Standard Time zone, so "noon" CST happened about thirty minutes before "high noon" in Dodge City.

Vin, the engineer for the ATSF local between Dodge City and Garden City, Kansas, arrived at the depot a little after 6:00 A.M. CST. His fireman, Percy, had already lit the fire in engine 1704 and was watching patiently as the engine came to life. Steam engines started cold had to be brought up to temperature and pressure slowly to avoid cracks in the boiler or firebox.

Percy was an expert at his job, and Vin was very happy to have him firing the engine. They would make the Dodge City to Garden City run and return today with stops in Cimarron both ways. The departure from Dodge City was scheduled for 8:15 A.M. "standard" time.

Engine 1704 would be pulling a coach car, a couple of boxcars, and a livestock car, plus a caboose.

Vin's crew consisted of Percy, the fireman; Tom, the conductor; Bill, the head brakeman; and Chuck, the rear brakeman. ATSF also assigned a couple of flagmen to go with 1704. They would be riding in the caboose with Chuck when not on the ground.

Vin and Percy would spend most of their time in the cab of the engine. Bill would be there also, but sometimes he had to leave the cab when they changed trains, moved switches or loaded freight cars.

Tom actually ran the train. The conductor was responsible for all movement of the train. He also checked passenger tickets and kept the logbooks. If the train was late, the conductor got the blame. If it was early, the engineer was praised.

Chuck and the flagmen rode in the caboose. Chuck watched the cars from the cupola and kept a lookout for hot wheel bearings. He and Bill were responsible for keeping the wheel bearings greased on every car in the train, so overheating didn't happen.

"Morning, Tom," Vin said when he entered the dispatcher's office.

"Morning, Vin. I got our track orders. The track is ours all the way to Garden City. Then we have to stay off the main center track until the westbound *Chief* passes through. That should happen around 11:30 A.M. Once the *Chief* clears Garden City, the track is ours again until 6:00 P.M. That's when the eastbound *Chief* comes through Dodge City." Vin knew all this already, but the conductor had to cover all track movements and track warrants before each run.

"We should be back here by then, so I don't see a problem."

"Yeah. How's Percy coming with the fire?"

"I didn't see any problems when I came by the shop. He'll let us know if there is, though."

"The train leaves at 8:15. Let's have the crew meeting at 7:45 right here." Tom pointed to the floor in the dispatcher's office.

"I'll let everybody know."

Vin checked his watch with Tom and the dispatcher before leaving the depot and walking to the siding where 1704 was sitting. After climbing up into the cab, Vin checked all the gauges and watched Percy toss another shovel full of coal into the firebox.

Percy nodded at Vin and picked up another shovel full of coal. Vin looked at his pocket watch. It was about

6:30 A.M., and the sun wasn't close to being up yet.

After tossing the coal into the firebox, Percy said, "Everything's looking good."

"Thanks. We'll move to the depot track at 7:15 and hook up. Crew meeting is 7:45."

Percy checked his watch and nodded. Percy was a man of few words, and that was okay. He and Vin had worked together a couple of years now, and they didn't need to say much to each other.

Bill joined Vin as they walked around the locomotive. Both had oil cans and took turns oiling the bearings on the wheels, side rods, and timing gear.

"Last week, robbers stopped the *Chief* outside of Lamar and made off with payroll money and mail. Wounded the conductor. What do you make of that?"

"Nothing good. We need to put more railroad police on the *Chief* between Wichita and Lamar. In the past, the bosses assumed the train crew would be able to see the robbers coming and be ready for them. Last week, the robbers proved how good they could hide. We don't have to worry about train robbers, though. The local train doesn't carry a lot of money and never any mail."

While Vin and Bill were checking the locomotive,

Tom and Chuck checked the train. The passenger car was clean and ready. Any passengers that arrived yesterday on the westbound local were required to remove all possessions and find lodging for the night. The boxcars were loaded, and someone swept out the livestock car.

"At least, the stink won't be so bad in the caboose heading to Garden City today."

"Yeah, but we'll have a full car for the return trip."

"Don't remind me!"

At 7:15, the pressure was up enough for 1704 to make the move to the depot track. Vin set the brakes on the locomotive while Bill pulled the chocks from the wheels. Steam locomotives did not have hand brakes so, when not under pressure, chocks were used to keep them from rolling.

Bill tossed the chocks into a side storage box and climbed on board for the short run to the depot track. First, they had to drive past the depot, then flip a switch and back up to the passenger car and hook up.

Tom and Chuck were waiting for them and guided them into position. Once the air hose was connected, Bill, Chuck and Tom walked the train and checked the brakes on each car. When the air brake testing was complete,

Vin set the train brakes, and all the hand brakes on the train were released, except the one on the caboose. While the track looked level to the casual observer, it wasn't. It sloped slightly downhill toward the locomotive. If the rear brakeman released the hand brakes on the caboose, all the cars would roll forward a little, putting slack in the couplers that would create a jolt when the locomotive started forward. This wasn't too bad for the passenger car, since it was right behind the locomotive, but the crew in the caboose could get a good jolt if all the slack was taken out quickly.

A yardman climbed into the cab to watch over everything while Vin, Percy and Bill joined Tom and Chuck in the dispatch office for the crew meeting.

At 8:00 A.M. CST, Tom called for passenger boarding. He did a cursory check to see if they had tickets as they boarded and would finish the ticketing process after the train was moving.

About 8:10, Tom and Chuck checked the boxcars to make sure the doors were closed and no one had hopped in looking for a free ride. After that, Tom checked with the dispatcher to make sure the track was still theirs. Then he waved a lantern at Vin.

It was still dark enough for the lantern to be more effective than waving a flag. This was the signal for Vin to begin their westbound movement.

Vin pulled the Johnson bar to set the timing about halfway, then cracked the throttle. Steam started to flow to the cylinders. Vin pulled the rope for the steam whistle twice sharply, to let the train crew know that they were about to start moving forward. He eased off the air brakes, and the locomotive started to move. The remaining slack in the couplers was taken up, and Chuck spun the hand brake wheel on the caboose to release it.

Bill was hanging out the side of the cab, looking for a signal from the caboose. One of the flagmen waved a flag at Bill to let him know that all the cars in the train were moving. Bill passed this on to Vin, and Vin cracked the throttle open a little more.

The run from Dodge City to Cimarron was only nineteen miles, but it would take them almost forty minutes to get there. There was a nice wind from the south that crossed over the Arkansas River before crossing the track. This would keep the smoke and cinders away from the cab and the passenger car.

Tom punched tickets after the train was clear of the station and chatted with everyone on board. Most were getting off at Garden City or Cimarron, but a few were ticketed all the way to Lamar. It would be a long ride for the Lamar passengers, and they would not arrive until sometime tomorrow. The *Chief* would get them there tonight, but it didn't stop in Dodge City. So, if you wanted to get to Lamar, you had to ride the local train or back-track to Wichita.

Right on time at 8:55, Vin pulled the train to a stop at Cimarron. They had thirty-five minutes for boarding passengers and moving freight off and on the boxcars. Vin and Bill checked the locomotive and oiled the bearings. Tom checked the passengers off the train, then checked with the dispatcher.

"The *Chief* left Wichita right on time and should pass through here at 11:00, as scheduled," the dispatcher said.

"That's what we heard. Thanks. How many passengers are we picking up?"

"Three for Garden City and two more for Lamar."

"Let 'em know that we'll board at 9:20, assuming the freight is ready by then."

"Can do."

Bill, Chuck and the flagmen were busy watching the unloading and loading of the freight. It didn't take long, and the boxcar doors were closed at 9:15.

Tom stepped into the station and said loudly, "All aboard for Garden City. Please have your tickets ready." Tom stepped back outside and lent a hand to anyone needing assistance getting on the train.

Chuck checked the boxcars one more time and waved to Tom that he was ready. At 9:30, Tom waved to Vin, and they were off for Garden City. *So far, so good*, thought Tom as he punched the tickets of the new passengers.

An hour and fifteen minutes later, 1704 pulled onto a siding near the station at Garden City. Before parking at the depot, they had to uncouple the livestock car and leave it on a siding.

Chuck set the hand brake on the caboose and pulled the uncoupling handle on the livestock car while waving for Vin to move the train forward. When the air hose between the livestock car separated, there was a pop and hiss. Chuck followed the train to the next switch and signaled Vin to stop the train once it was clear.

Chuck flipped the switch and signaled Vin to back the train into a different siding. Once the livestock car was set on the siding where it was supposed to be, the hand brakes were set, and Chuck uncoupled it from the train.

Vin and Chuck repeated the process in reverse and picked up the caboose before pulling up to the platform at the depot. They'd be busy here, since this was where they unhooked from the remainder of the train, added coal and water, turned the locomotive around, hooked up to the eastbound cars and took a lunch break. They had two hours to take care of all this, which was plenty of time, and they had to wait for the *Chief* to pass through.

Bill, Chuck and the flagmen set the hand brakes on the passenger car and box cars before uncoupling the locomotive.

Again, there was a pop and hiss as the air hose disconnected. The hand brakes had better hold, or the train would roll away. They did.

The eastbound train was ready on the third track. The *Chief* would have the center track when it came through. Passengers boarding the eastbound train would have to climb the stairs to an overhead walkway that crossed over all three tracks when it was time to board.

Vin, Percy and Bill drove the locomotive out of the station with Bill moving switches to place 1704 on the track heading to the turntable and roundhouse. Bill had to reset the switches once 1704 was past.

This was an "arm-strong" turntable, meaning Bill and a helper had to unlock the turntable and spin it around by hand, pushing and pulling the handles to make it rotate to the desired track and with 1704 pointing the correct direction.

Bill lined up 1704 with the siding that led to the coaling tower and water tower. They didn't get a lunch break until the locomotive's tender was full of water and coal and coupled to the eastbound train.

Meanwhile, Tom and Chuck were checking the cars on the eastbound track. It rolled into Garden City, minus the livestock car, not long before they arrived, and Chuck wanted to make sure they didn't inherit any hot bearings. The previous crew had to switch in the livestock car before they got their lunch break. This was already done. Sometimes, things moved fast and according to schedule on the railroad.

Once 1704 was attached to the eastbound train, a yardman took over in the cab while Vin, Percy and Bill took their lunch break. The yardman would keep the fire going and the pressure up while everyone was eating.

The livestock car was loaded with Texas Longhorn cattle from a ranch not far from Garden City. All the longhorn cattle coming from Texas were driven directly to Dodge City or Abilene. These longhorns were from a ranch out west of Garden City. Rather than drive them to Dodge City, the rancher had made arrangements with ATSF to pick them up in Garden City instead. That's why they hauled an empty livestock car out to Garden City.

This only happened once a week and would end soon, once the rancher had shipped all the cattle he could afford to ship. The last scheduled shipment was next week, so they would not bring an empty car out but would pick up the one they just dropped off and take it back.

Chuck wasn't too happy about having a cattle car right in front of the caboose, but it was only once a week, and it helped pay his salary.

A little after 11:30, the *Chief* rolled through the station on the center track between both eastbound and westbound trains. A mailbag was hanging on the pickup hook, and the grappling arm from the mail car snagged it easily.

A mailman on the *Chief* tossed another mail bag onto the platform between the center track and the inside track. The station master kept this platform clear of people when the *Chief* was coming through, just for this reason.

At 12:15, the westbound passengers were loaded, and their train left the station. At 12:45, the eastbound passengers were loaded and 1704 departed the station. Halfway back to Cimarron, Chuck started smelling something he didn't like. It was the smell of a hot bearing, and he had to get the attention of the locomotive crew, in order to get the train stopped. Chuck leaned out the cupola window and started waving a red flag back and forth trying to attract the attention of the engineer. At first, no one noticed this, so Chuck had one of the flagmen climb on top of the caboose and wave another flag. This finally got Bill's attention, and he called for Vin to stop the train.

After the train was stopped, Bill and Vin left the cab and started walking back toward the caboose. Vin climbed into the passenger car and told Tom what was going on. Both assumed that they had a hot bearing, and both were correct. Vin got back on the ground and followed Bill to the livestock car where Chuck and one of the flagmen were looking at the front truck.

"We got a hot one here," Chuck yelled to Vin as he got closer. The cattle were not happy with the smell and were making a lot of noise.

Chuck wasn't happy, either.

Besides having to smell cow shit all the way back to Dodge City, he now had to nursemaid a stinking hot bearing as well.

"I'll stuff it with grease, and we'll see how it holds up. Let's go slow for a bit, then I'll add more grease." Chuck told Vin, like Vin had never heard this before, but they still needed to say it.

Chuck pried the grease cover up and waved his hand at the smoke like that was going to help. The flagman had already retrieved a grease bag from the caboose and tossed it into the grease carrier. The wheel bearings were brass sleeves, and they were greased by a screw action that pulled the grease from the carrier on the end of the axle into the bearing. Without grease, the bearings would overheat and melt. If they had been damaged somehow, they could overheat, even with grease, and that would burn the grease out. Chuck was hoping that the fresh grease would cool the bearing enough to allow them to finish the run back to Dodge City.

When Vin and Bill returned to the locomotive, Chuck was already waving for them to start moving.

Vin put in a little timing and a little throttle.

Once the air brakes were released, the train started moving. Chuck and the flagman walked alongside the livestock car watching the hot bearing. A quarter of a mile or so later, the bearing had stopped smoking, and Chuck waved for Vin to stop the train. Bill relayed this as Chuck was on Bill's side of the train.

Another grease bag was tossed into the carrier, and Chuck waved for the train to start moving again. Chuck and the flagman watched the bearing for another half-mile before deciding it might be okay. They slowed down and let the caboose catch up to them. First, the flagman jumped on, then Chuck did. If either missed the jump, Vin would have to stop the train, but both made it aboard. Chuck then leaned out where Bill could see him and waved the flag to signal that they could proceed.

Vin knew that this still meant going slower than normal. They would arrive in Cimarron late and even later in Dodge City. Chuck packed more grease into the livestock carrier in Cimarron, and it looked like it would make the trip.

Once back in Dodge City, the yard crew would have to replace this bearing and maybe the axle also.

At Cimarron, the dispatcher telegraphed Dodge City to let them know what was going on with 1704 and when they pulled out for Dodge City. Vin and his crew pulled into Dodge City almost two hours late but well ahead of the eastbound *Chief*. Another successful day on the railroad for Vin and crew and for ATSF; both east and westbound *Chief*s made the journey without problems.

ROSEMARIE DURGIN

THE NEW HATBAND

Rosemarie Durgin was born just before WWII in Germany. She came to America in 1963 and is the mother of four and grandmother of ten. Writing has always been her strong suit, and she has wanted to write since childhood. Now that she is retired, she writes almost full time, with two of her novels to be published shortly. Besides writing, Rosemarie enjoys traveling, reading, needlework, wildlife and photography. Rosemarie lives with her husband John in Bethany, Oklahoma, with a menagerie of cats and dogs.

THE NEW HATBAND

by Rosemarie Durgin

Billy Underwood was clearing brush on the land his pa was homesteading not far from Fort Griffin in north central Texas near the little town of Albany in Shackelford County. They had left Tennessee for Texas not long after the war between the States had ended, once Pa had returned, and it had become clear that the Northern carpetbaggers were going to make them into penniless losers. So they had set out for the promised land - Texas!

Pa was planting cedar posts over near the house, so they could string the new barbed wire to keep the cattle contained. Billy was clearing another meadow of mesquite, so the grass would have a chance to grow on this brutally hot July day.

They had been in Shackelford County on this land for almost four years now. At first, they had been down around Jefferson. Ma had liked it there, but all the good land around there was taken, and jobs had been hard to find, so they had moved on to the Fort Griffin area.

If things went well, in another year, the land would

be theirs, and they would have more land, more than they had back in Tennessee.

Billy remembered the journey well. He was just a little tyke then of a little more than three years. Now he was about grown up, a man of just thirteen years old.

Billy was awakened from his reverie by the bellowing of the calf that was grazing not too far away. What was all that about? He looked over in the direction of the calf but could see nothing that would threaten the little cow, so he continued with his chore, but the calf would not stop bellowing.

I best go and see what that is all about. I can't see any coyote or cat that might cause this kind of trouble, he thought. He put down his tools and rushed over to where the calf was standing, stock still, not moving. On the way, he picked up some of the rocks lying about, hoping to chase off whatever was bothering the calf. Nearing the critter, he still could not see any kind of danger, but the little heifer was standing stock still and bellowing and was wild eyed; that much was for certain.

And then he heard it. The unmistakeable rattle of a Diamondback sidewinder. The snake lay curled up on a large, flat rock outcropping, ready to strike with its rattle up and head up, ready to hurl itself at its enemy.

The snake knew, it could not ingest the cow. Its heat sensors had told it, the prey was much too large. But the snake also knew that the sharp hooves of the cow would be able to injure him, if not kill him. The cow was still too young to know that.

Billy knew that in this heat and lying on this hot rock, the snake would be very fast indeed. Why can this not be a cold January day? Then the snake would be very sluggish, if mobile, at all. More likely, it would be hibernating in its hole someplace waiting for warmer weather.

Billy hurled one of his rocks at the snake, after having noted that the snake was hungry. There was no bulge near his head, where a partially ingested meal might be lodged and waiting to be fully digested. He missed!

The rock landed a couple of feet in front of the snake, but that movement had attracted the snake's attention, and the second rock hit it square in the head.

The snake lay stunned, and Billy completed its demise by pounding its head repeatedly with a third and larger missile. The snake was immobile.

It was time to lead the little heifer to safety. She did

not want to move, but Billy was able to cajole her to come toward the barn.

It took a long time to calm the animal down, to where Billy was able to make her move as he wanted her to. Before walking the little cow home, though, Billy first checked her over, to make sure she had not been bitten by the snake. He ran his hands over all her legs, checking for swelling or a tender spot or even a small speck of blood. He could not find anything, the same with her sides and head. Once he had searched her body thoroughly, he was satisfied the calf had not been bitten by the poisonous serpent, and he was able to move her towards the barn.

That evening, Billy's father wanted to know why he had left his chores and returned to the house so early in the day? He was right upset with his son.

"I told you not to play. We have to get that pasture cleared before the next batch of calves is born. You are almost ready to strike out on your own. At that rate, you are never going to be of much account," he scolded his son.

"Pa, I had to take the heifer to the barn. She was frightened to death by that sidewinder."

"What did you do with the snake?"

"I left it there; I was taking care of the heifer."

"Go get it. We can't afford to let good meat go to waste."

"Pa, it's a snake, a poisonous snake. We can't eat that."

"What do you think you have been eating every morning for the last four years with your eggs?"

"Meat, not snake!"

"Snake, that's good eating. Go get it before the coyotes come and take it."

Billy had no choice but to do as he was told. He took along a pillow sheet into which to stick the carcass. He was not going to touch that slimy beast. On the way, he found himself a stout forked stick, with which to pick the snake up.

When Billy got back to the rock outcropping where he had left the snake, the sun was going down, and the day had cooled considerably.

A thunderstorm was threatening; lightning was already flashing across the sky, and thunder could be heard. The snake was still where he had left it. To his dismay, the beast was not dead but barely moving.

Billy was able to finish it off this time, but he had to

touch the serpent as he put it into the sack.

To his surprise, the snake was not slimy at all. It was dry and a bit scaly, but not slimy, and it was beautiful. While he was away, it had completed shedding. The skin was still attached to the last rattle. Billy realized why he had been able to almost kill the critter then, without being bitten himself. The snake could not see properly. The old skin was still attached to its head, making its vision blurry. Now he felt bad for killing the creature, but he shook himself. It was just a snake, a vermin, a beast they had to exterminate from their land, to make it safe for all.

When Billy got back to the ranch house, it was dark and had started to rain in earnest.

CR&O

A few weeks later on his birthday, Billy received as a present from his parents: a new straw hat. Around its crown was a beautiful, new, snakeskin hatband.

Billy was stunned. That hatband was more expensive than the entire hat. He could not believe his parents had spent so much of their hard earned and scarce coins on him.

"Oh, that hatband cost nothing." his mother told him. "We made it from the skin of the snake you killed a while back."

DEBBIE FOGLE

HERE LIES LESTER SMECK

Debbie Fogle is a member of Romance Writers of America and the OKRWA Chapter and was a judge for the 2016 International Digital awards. She is the author of *Happiness is Hard to Find,* published by hybrid publisher iUniverse. She also has several short stories published with Kindness Publications and Creative Quills. She currently resides in Blanchard, OK.

HERE LIES LESTER SMECK

by Debbie Fogle

Oklahoma in August of 1908. The tailor shop is his pride and joy. The tailor shop is also his moneymaker and livelihood. *There is a God*, he believes, when he realizes he is the only tailor in a one hundred mile radius.

"Truly blessed, I am, indeed," he declares as he switches the sign to "open".

He grew up in Pauls Valley, Oklahoma. Lance and his brothers were raised in the building in which he now lives and works. For some reason, he doesn't remember his childhood, other than constantly working and helping his mother with the material and notions for the making of linens and clothing. His father would stomp around the house, "Mabel, these boys don't need to be learnin' that sewing stuff. They need to be outside learnin' man stuff." This statement would be followed by a strong slap on Lance's back.

Why his father named him Lance Arlington Vance boggles his mind. You can't give your son a name like that and expect him to make friends. Lance was thankful he didn't have to attend school very much.

He learned all about calculations and comprehension from his mother. Every inch of fabric and ribbons was measured to the mark. Taking instructions for the items to be made had to be written down precisely to the customers' satisfaction.

His mother, bless her soul, made everyone happy with her intricate designs. Lance is proud he has carried on the tradition of a professional tailor in his mother's name. Lance's mother would make anything and everything. Lance makes men's clothing, and that is it.

He stokes the fire to get a warm temperature in the store. Stoking the fire also preps his coffee pot and heats up the pressing irons. He walks back to the window, opens the curtains to let the sunlight in. Lance notices two gentlemen standing by the banister. Those men are not from this area. The suits they are wearing are made of wool, not a cotton blend. The men are definitely from up North. Lance is positive these men will make his day interesting.

The bell on the tailor shop door chimes.

"Good morning, sirs, may I help y'all?" Lance greets in his Oklahoma slang.

"We would like to have some special suits made," the short, pudgy gentleman states.

"Well, my man," Lance begins to walk over to his mannequins, "all of my suits are special, Sir. You'll have to be more specific. Is there a certain color you're looking for?" Lance takes the bait.

The tall stranger steps forward, "We want to have suits made to carry items." The tall man pats his breast pocket on his wool blend jacket. Sweat beads are glistening on the man's forehead.

Lance can see these two men are already uncomfortable in their wool suits. The temperature is warm outside, and the tailor shop is the same temperature as it is outside. What is the real reason these two strangers have wandered into the only tailor shop in Pauls Valley, Oklahoma?

"Do you need a pocket mended? Or some extra stitching on your lapels?" Lance begins the word play with the two men.

The pudgy man removes his felt hat in frustration, steps forward, and blurts out, "We want one of your special suits!"

"Sir, as I stated earlier, all of my suits are special.

Do you need a suit for a formal event? A suit for an outdoor event? If you plan on going on a ranch or the range, may I suggest you invest in some of those Levi Strauss trousers? I hear those denim jeans are most excellent on wear and tear for the outside activities." Lance knows he's hitting nerves with both men.

"Did you know those Levis have been around since 1873?" Lance adds just for the hell of it.

"We will return later!" the tall man declares as he reaches for the solid glass door knob.

"That will be wonderful. I will get out some designs you may be interested in. You should really check out those Levis at the Mercantile Store." Lance is smiling as he walks to the entrance door of the tailor shop. He walks out into the Oklahoma sunshine with the two men.

"Have a nice day gentlemen," he greets. Under his breath, he adds, "I'm not that stupid. Have fun sweating your asses off." He walks to his register and enters two numbers on a small chalkboard behind the register. This will show his regular customers of the alert that has been recorded.

His clientele are the most professional, trustworthy customers in the state of Oklahoma. During these trying

trying times, it's hard to find true and honest people. The two men that have left his shop are not trustworthy. He's positive they work for the ASL, which means he'll be very slow today. Once word gets around about those two men, distribution will slow to a halt.

Prior to 1907 statehood, Oklahoma and Indian territories (the Twin Territories) had different liquor policies. Oklahoma Territory (O.T.) laws permitted the sale of alcohol, but in Indian Territory (I.T.) federal laws prohibited the distribution of intoxicants. For more than a decade before statehood, the powerful Anti-Saloon League (ASL) and the Women's Christian Temperance Union (WCTU) forces waged war against the legalized sale of liquor on O.T. and called for stricter enforcement in I.T.

As statehood neared, prohibitionists, with Protestant churches as their key support, flexed the political muscle to select Constitutional Convention delegates who would frame an anti-liquor law into the new state's constitution.

Lance is against this law. He enjoys his brandy, whiskey and a beer on social occasions. Sometimes, he enjoys all of the throat burning liquors in one evening, depending on his attitude.

Today, the risk becomes fact. The fact is: he's about to lose his family business, the business his mother struggled to create with his father struggling to make sure his mother was happy. He can't lose the tailor shop over a few secret pockets. He'll wait to hear from his customers to determine his next move. In the meantime, he opens his front doors to show he has nothing to hide.

Lance begins his work: tailoring six pairs of trousers, four skirted overcoats, nine raincoats, twenty-two shirts, one Norfolk jacket, and he preps two hats. He will send the hats out to the milliner. Lance doesn't like dealing with hat making. He prepares the fabric to match the customer vests and then runs the products over to the milliner. Business is good.

BOOM!

He hears a loud bang at the back of his shop. He runs through the small rooms to the back of his shop. He reaches the mud room to see his back door on fire.

"FIRE!" he hears someone yelling in the alleyway.

He turns around, exiting the mud room. He closes the sealed doors that separate the pressing room from the mud room.

He runs through the tailor shop, closing each door to contain the smoke damage, thanking his mother for installing the special doors in 1896.

"FIRE IN THE ALLEY!" he yells out.

Immediately, people on the streets grab what they can and begin to form a line, each one grabbing a bucket and passing the bucket over to the next person. One person is filling the buckets with water at the pump. There is no stopping a community of citizens that bond together. He knows each one of these people will risk their lives to help him, and he would do the same for them. By the way things are looking, he may be risking a lot more today.

The fire is doused, but some damage has been done. Some smoke has traveled into his pressing area and contaminated some stored fabric. The sheriff and fire marshal arrive to talk with Lance about the incident.

He gives his statement, declaring he truly doesn't know who would do such a thing to his shop. The fire marshall informs Lance that the fire seems to have been started with a combination of moonshine and lamp oil.

"Oh, the secret message," Lance thinks to himself.

"Mr. Vance," the sheriff begins, "keep us informed of anyone suspicious. We will catch the person responsible for this." The sheriff shakes Lance's hand and leaves Lance looking at the damages at the back door of his shop.

So you want to play? Lance brushes off the ashes from his shirt and vest. His mother has shown him how to sew, but his father taught him the art of defense. His father once employed a Chinese man servant. Lin was trained in combative defense. Lance was taught by a great master of the art of war. When Lance showed his father he could be a tailor with a special talent, his father was proud.

"Mr. Vance," the milliner calls out.

"Are you all right, sir?" asks a concerned townsman.

"Yes, I'm all right, Mr. Russell. Our meeting tonight will be interesting." Lance attempts to close the half-burned door, but it crumbles from the movement. He will ask the locksmith and builder to come over and repair the damaged door. He will pay some Chinese girls to clean the pressing room.

The fire won't break Lance's bank account. The fire is the work of an ignorant man who thinks this act will scare Lance, an ignorant man that thinks Lance is nothing but a tailor.

"Lance Arlington Vance!" a sultry voice calls out.

"Holly, dear, you shouldn't be around all this mess. It could be dangerous." He speaks his concern, but his eyes are drinking in her beauty.

Holly stands before him wearing a simple dress and bonnet. Her blonde locks of hair are streaming like gold from under the bonnet. He loves the woman standing before him. Her father has already given his blessing for the marriage proposal that he was planning tomorrow night. The two strangers in town had better not mess with his plans.

"Lance Arlington Vance, don't try to fool me. I know what is going on. I saw those two goons walking through town. You forget who I'm in love with." Smiling, her eyes sparkle.

He's embarrassed by his assumption. She's not the porcelain doll that will break when dropped. She's like a solid wall of cast iron, and she's beautiful. He knows, because he's been training her for the last three years. She too can fight, if need be.

"A-hum." She clears her throat, knowing a devious thought is going through his mind.

He leans over to kiss her. "Sorry, my love. Please return to your place, and I will see you later," knowing deep in his heart he wants to hold her till eternity.

The dry road in town allows her to stroll easily toward home. The summer heat is coming to an end. Fall will soon be here, and there will be many changes happening in the next year.

Heat from the ASL and the WCTU is trickling down to Pauls Valley, Oklahoma. Holly is prepared for these situations that may arise. She's no fool. She knows the man she's in love with isn't just a tailor. She knows he loves his country, his God, and her.

The two strangers are at the hotel restaurant planning to have a nice, home-cooked lunch.

"He's a lying scab," the pudgy man declares.

"Ssssshhhhh," the tall man orders, as he takes a drink of water. "You need to keep your voice down, Lester."

"Keep quiet?" Lester blurts out, then realizes he's gathered the attention of everyone in the restaurant.

The tall man leans over the table. He gently inserts the tips of his fork into the top of Lester's right hand. He applies slow pressure, penetrating Lester's skin. Lester feels the fork slowly digging into his flesh. He stops talking.

"Keep quiet," growls the tall man as he removes the fork and drops it on the floor.

"Sorry, Max. I'll keep quiet." Lester takes his cloth napkin and places the napkin over the small bleeding wounds.

A small girl walks by and retrieves the fork from the floor and returns with a napkin wrapped around another set of silverware.

Max and Lester eat in silence. Max is trying to think of a plan that won't include blowing up the whole town of Pauls Valley, Oklahoma. He wants to return to Yale, Michigan, where it's cold and quiet. He hates to travel long distances for work, but he's paid very well for the work he does.

"I'm here for my fitting, Lance." The sheriff walks in and stands with his arms straight out, to the side. "Were you able to make those special alterations we discussed?"

"Yes, here. Let's slip on your cutaway coat and see how the garment fits." Lance removes the gray cotton tweed coat and holds it out for the sheriff.

"Fits like a glove," the sheriff compliments. "How are you going to handle the two gents in town? One is packin'. You need to be careful. They could've burned your business down.

"If this building starts to burn, the whole town may damn well explode from all the liquid you have in your walls." He gestures to the small pipes that run along the solid brick walls of Lance's shop.

"I know. Those lines took me forever to rig up, but they work perfectly. Looking at them, you'd think I had running water." Lance gives a short guffaw. He finishes with the Sheriff's coat fitting and shakes his hand as they exit the shop.

"Till next time." The sheriff tips his hat and walks down the dirt road to his jail.

Lance is thinking of an old saying his father used to say: if it ain't broke, don't fix it. Lance doesn't like strangers coming to his town and breaking things. He's mad about the fire, and he's really mad about the smell of smoke in his pressing room. He will take pride in rectifying this situation.

Lester and Max finish their meals and decide to check out the local shops, stopping here and there for some supplies needed for their next job. Max makes a mental list and will stop at every store to find what he needs. After shopping, Lester and Max head over to the church.

BOOM!

The explosion sends a pillar of smoke up from the side of the church. People run frantically to the house of God. Once again, the line of water-carriers form, and the task is complete. One side of the church is severely damaged.

Holly is covered in ash, and her dress is black from the smoke. She walks into her home next to the church.

"Your father shouldn't have flammable liquids near his church," the snarling voice declares.

Holly turns around, facing the two strangers. "How dare you set fire to my father's church!" she accuses.

"I like your spunk." The tall stranger steps toward Holly and grabs her wrist.

The pudgy man spits tobacco on the hem of Holly's dress. "Maybe we can have some fun," he insinuates.

The movement of Holly's leg happens so fast that Lester doesn't know what hits him. His neck snaps within a millisecond. The palm of her hand hit Max's neck with so much force, he begins gasping for air. Max runs out the door to the outskirts of town. Max is still running as Lance walks up next to Holly and takes her hand into his.

Max's body has never been found. The coyotes of Oklahoma must have devoured it. It's like contributing to the circle of life.

As a warning to any other agents that want to investigate the goings-on in this region, Lester is buried at the small cemetery two miles before you get to Pauls Valley. On Lester's tombstone, it clearly states: HERE LIES LESTER SMECK – DIED OF A BROKEN NECK.

ANDREA FOSTER

THE MEANING OF NOTHING

Andrea Foster is an editor and author who has been in the book business since 1977. She currently teaches Writing and Composition at Redlands Community College, Creative Writing at the Carnegie Library in El Reno, and How to Write, Publish & Market Your Book at the Canadian Valley Technology Center, CVTech. She has been published in various magazines and newspapers. She currently resides in Kingfisher, OK.

THE MEANING OF NOTHING

by Andrea Foster

Raney Blaine was a doer, not a thinker. Now, that's not to say he didn't do some ponderin' now and again, but he tended to save that kinda thinkin' for when he was savorin' one of his hand-rolled quirleys—or for when he was havin' a shot of that prairie dew. When drinkin', he liked to roll the whiskey around in his mouth and on his tongue and suck it through his teeth down the back of his throat with a sound like a hissing snake. SSSSLLLLLPPPPP!

Just now he'd finished rolling his tobacco in a perfectly dried cornhusk, and he was about to light it with a striker and have a good smoking meditation. That was Raney's time to consider, and if he didn't want to think about somethin', he'd blow smoke rings and watch them vanish in the air to nothin', avoiding the somethin' he was s'posed to be considerin'. But this time, there was no avoiding it.

His pal Vance Gann had slipped up. He'd always knowed he shouldn'ta trusted Vance, 'cause Vance had that way about him.

Vance always was a bit of a barber's clerk—that's a fella who likes to fancy himself a gentle-man. Those as knowed him knowed he was really a bit of a porch percher. But nobody had never took him for a chiseler, and now Raney was purty dang sure that his pal Vance Gann was indeed a snake. Still 'n' all, Raney was disappointed. He had knowed Vance since they were kids. Because o' that, Raney had always been willing to give Vance every opportunity, and when Vance offered his childhood friend a chance to stake a claim in Colorada, Raney said to himself, "Why not?" He knowed he'd probably have to sit on Vance to git 'im to work, but how hard would that be if'n there were no floozies to get sweet on and no hard bit saloons to hear tell of out in the wilds?

Truth be told, Vance did work hard, hardest Raney'd ever seen him work, and they had prospered. At first. They hadn't hit the mother lode, but they were doin' well enough and kept busy and slowly amassed a nice bit of gold sand and a few nuggets.

Then Raney noticed that Vance began to get slower and slower, and oftentimes, he'd find Vance sittin' in the shade, rolling a quirley, lookin' a bit crazy eyed and antsy.

"You all right, Vance?" he'd ask, and Vance'd reply, "Sure, sure," and hesitantly get his rear end up to start diggin' again.

Then, one day, Raney noticed Vance all afiddlin' with his horse and saddle and lookin' around all nervous like. He 'bout jumped out of his skin when Raney said, "Whater ya up to there, Vance?"

"Nuthin', nuthin'. I jest can't take it here no more, Raney. I just got to go find me a town and get m'self a good meal n' a girl n' some good conversatin'."

"Well, I know I'm not much of a chatterbox," Raney'd admitted, bowing his head.

"No, no, jest let me go fer a bit, 'n' I'll be back in a few days, and you can hold the claim."

"Aw right then," Raney'd replied. He didn't mind bein' alone. He kinda liked not havin' to talk to anybody, even Vance, who he'd knowed 'bout all his life. "Right, then. See ya."

Vance rode away on his little mare, and Raney'd noticed that the further he went, the more he sped up.

Now as I said, Raney Blaine was a doin' man, not a thinker, and suddenly, he'd hankered to roll a quirley so's he could ponder the situation.

Like, why did Vance speed up to make his get away? Raney carefully spread the tobacco from his pouch, Rolled the husk paper with the flourish of one who's done it often, and lit the end. He drew in the smoke, swirled it in his mouth, and blew out a long swooshing curlicue of smoke. And he got to considerin'.

Why would Vance Gann rush out of here like a man chased when he had a whole cache of gold buried under that there rock? Raney leaned on his knees and looked across the site to the big boulder they'd named "The Bank". That's when Raney saw the dirt around it was hastily thrown about, and was he mistaken, or did the boulder look a bit out of place? That's when Raney jumped up, the quirley butt chomped between his teeth, and ran to the boulder. The Bank. The Bank had been moved. Raney began to dig with his hands. Did Vance? No--did Vance? Oh, no. Vance did. Vance robbed The Bank. Did he take it all? Vance did. That hard fisted little chiseler.

Raney sat on the ground, dirt strewn in his lap, teeth still tightly clamped on the quirley that had sputtered out and gone cold. Raney felt his heart go cold, too. He was mad as a hornet. He felt mockered, used.

If Vance were here, Raney'd sure want to invite 'im to a necktie party—his own! But Raney wasn't gonna go after him. Vance wasn't worth goin' after.

Besides, Raney didn't want to lose the claim. If he left, somebody else could come in there and take over. He knew this was good here. He couldn't take the chance. No, better to let that no-count owl hoot of a Vance Gann be gone, and jest let him try to come back and re-take the claim. He jest bought his name off the claim. Raney got up and checked for his gun and rifle, still here, still loaded. He might have to use them, if the chiseler came back. Then Raney used the striker to relight his cigarette. He leaned against a tree and finished savoring the tobacco, contemplatin' a scenario he hoped would never happen, and then he threw the butt down and got back to doin'.

A few months later, Raney was packing away his latest take and squirreling it away in a new location. That other "bank" was closed for business, and there was a new place in town.

Raney, now that he'd been alone, worked more rather than less, with no other persons to keep 'im company or require his attention. Raney worked morning, noon, and night—yes, in the moonlight, he often worked.

His rations were getting mighty low, though, and he was going to have to give it up and go to town for provisions, but he surely didn't look forward to doin' that.

He'd gotten a bit paranoid about leaving the claim, and he sure 'nough didn't want to run into Vance Gann anywheres. Instead, he started eating less and less, and he was gettin' skinny as a rail, and his energy was flagging. He knew he was going to have to give it up, but he had become like a man obsessed. A man obsessed with diggin'. He had almost made back the amount that Vance had stolen, and he was determined to outdo that before he left his post, but it was gettin' harder and harder.

As I said, Raney was packing away his latest haul and hiding it under carefully disarranged branches, rocks and wood, when he heard the crackle of hooves on brush and leaves. The weather was getting cooler, and really, Raney had wanted to stay at the claim until the first snow hid his diggin' hole, but apparently, he was goin' to have a visitor.

Raney moved to his horse, which whinnied a welcome to the coming animal and rider, and he pulled out his rifle.

"Raney!" came the familiar voice. "Raney! You still out here?" Horse and rider had slowed to approach, trying to view the situation.

Raney positioned himself on the other side of his pony, with one hand on his rifle, and the other on the back of the animal. Vance Gann rode slowly forward on a new steed, with a pack donkey behind him. He rode up and jumped off quickly.

"Hey, Raney! I got the provisions!" he called, taking off his hat and brushin' down his new city slicker clothes. He stood up straight and looked at Raney with a shifty look, tryin' to be Mr. Cheer, all right. It was just like Vance to pull a fast one and then pretend like nuthin' had happened. He was slipperier than a hog in muck, fer sure.

Raney peered over his horse with narrowed eyes and said nothing, absolutely nothing.

"Raney, I got us the provisions, Raney. Got my hankerin' taken care of. Had my fling in town, 'n' now we're good to go, buddy!"

Vance was actin' like everything was normal; they were still pals, even after he'd robbed their Bank and taken all their hard money.

"I heared tell that more people were comin' this way, so I got us some grub and some extra fire power to protect our claim if'n anybody was to find us 'n' the claim."

Raney just looked at Vance, silent. He could feel his blood risin'. He needed to stay calm, though, and not go helter skelter, so he just stood, clamp-mouthed, eying his former partner.

"Look at this, Raney!" Vance pulled out a beautiful pearl handled pistol, like a kid in a penny candy store, all excited-like, wantin' to do show 'n' tell. "I got us some good lookin' protection here, some purty dang good fire power, bud! What're ya doin'? Ya don't look so good, Raney. Ya look mighty gnarly there. How 'bout we get us some grub? I got grub, Raney!"

"'N' how'd ya pay for it, Vance?" Raney finally spoke, tired. Tired of the same old song and dance he'd knowed all his life.

"Why, Raney, I had to use our scuds to pay for all this," he waved his arms around at the pack-laden mount and its saddlebags.

"Boy, am I stove up," he said walking around stiff legged, tryin' to stretch 'is timbers some, still a bit saddle stiff. That was Vance. Tryin' to change the subject when he knowed he done wrong. Tryin' ta act like nuthin's happened, when he'd just been served up as bein' a scalawag.

"You robbed The Bank, Vance." Raney was calm now, and focused.

"I didn't rob The Bank, Raney! That money was our'n, and I went to get provisions 'n'…"

"You said you'd be gone three days, Vance."

"Well, Raney, you know how it is. Ya go to town, get all sewed up with the firewater, play a few hands of cards, git yerself a spicy Jane. Next thing ya know, a week's gone by. You know how it is, Raney. I got yer some tabacca!" Vance started to dig in the pack, and Raney's hand tightened on his rifle and began to pull it to his chest.

"Vance, you said three days. It's been three months. Three months."

Raney's eyes narrowed more. Vance threw a package of tobacco under the pony's feet.

That was Vance, all right. Far as he was concerned, he ain't done nuthin'. Raney remembered somethin' his mama had said about Vance oncet, the first time Vance'd done something stupid and hurt his feelin's by bein' thoughtless. She'd said, "He don't mean nothin' by it, Raney. That's just his way."

But Raney had seen it his whole life.

Vance had been like a brother to him—a no-count brother, but still a brother. But this was the last straw.

"Where'd ya get those duds, Vance?"

"Why, Raney, y' know I had to get ragged proper, if'n I was ta get m'self a gal, you know that. 'N' I look good, don't I—ey, Raney? Ey?" Vance spread his arms and smiled like the big dumb cluck that he was, oblivious.

"Where's the rest of it, Vance?"

"Lookit all I got fer us, Raney. Here it all is!" Vance swept his arms around the scene: the horses, the pack animal, the load of provisions and other stuffs.

"Where's the rest of the money, Vance?"

Now, Vance started to panic, 'cause he saw that Raney was bein' single-minded about the gold and was not bein' appreciative of all the other loot he had brung 'im.

"Why, Raney, this is the money. The gold bought all this; that's now all for you. Whyn't we get us some grub, Raney? You look a bit sharp set, brother. Let's get us some jerky for now, and then get this all fired up and make yer some eggs 'n' a nice pot of bait with some of this here swamp seed. I'm all tuckered out, but I'll do it fer ya. You look knackered yerself."

Vance began to hustle about the campfire, somethin' he knew how to do but rarely did, 'cause he was too dang lazy. But he knew his rear end was on the line right now, and he had better make up for what he'd done.

Raney said nothing. He knew the money was gone. He could tell from the second he'd laid eyes on Vance in his new duds with new packs and unbroken leather and denim—Vance looked stiff as a board—Raney knowed the gold was gone. All of it. Else n' Vance wouldn't'a come back.

Raney took the tobacco, and Vance, while keepin' a vigilant eye on his wary benefactor, and anyways, bein' accomodatin', threw Raney a pack of rolling papers. Raney wanted to sigh at this tiny example of extravagance, but didn't.

He remained hard and cold as ice, picked up the papers and rolled hisself a quirley so's he could ponder. He didn't blow smoke holes, either. He contemplated real hard.

In the days that came, Vance worked real hard, like he was a changed man. He wadn't, though. He just knowed his gig was up and that Raney was still mad and still silent as a dormouse. Vance knowed he had to kiss up real hard to get back on Raney's good side. Vance became super-accomodatin'.

He became the man ever'body wished, all those years, that he could be. But as the weather got colder, he was gettin' madder too. Why wasn't his friend talkin' to him no more? Vance was workin'. What more did Raney want? Not only that, but Raney had his own Bank. Vance tried to figger out where it t'was, but that Raney'd become mighty sneaky since he'd been gone.

Vance found Raney worked all hours of the day and night, like one of them machines they had back in Chicagger. Sometimes, Vance'd wake to find Raney standin' over 'im, smokin' a quirley, that he, Vance, had paid for. Vance'd been the one to go to town and git all the stuff.

Raney wouldn't have nothin' if'n it weren't for me, thought Vance. Raney'd never even gone to Colorada, if Vance hadn'ta suggested it. Raney owed Vance that money he'd took from The Bank. Raney owed him.

The weather was gettin' mighty cold, and both men knew that the time to leave the claim would come soon. They threw theirselves into diggin' with a fervor, Raney diggin' a big trough off the track.

"What'r ya doin' that fer?" asked Vance, a bit irritated and wonderin' what kind of craziness his old friend had gotten into his knucklehead. "Didya hit a vein there?"

"Nope. Jest investigatin'." Raney was more tight-lipped than ever, since Vance'd come back. Raney was a doin' man, all right, but he'd set to ponderin' more and more as the weather got colder 'n' colder. He was grateful inside for the provisions Vance had brought, but he knowed that he'd paid for them hisself, not Vance. Vance had robbed The Bank, and Raney wadn't about ta forget. He watched Vance hustle around like he never had before, and he let Vance suck up to 'im. Vance owed 'im all that kissin' up—to pay off for a lifetime of triflin', stupid, thoughtless behavior.

The first snows came, and still the men huddled in their bedrolls, and still Raney would go diggin' at all hours of the day and night. Vance let 'im. Vance stayed by the fire more and more, spent more time pretendin' to cook and rustle up grub. They barely spoke.

Finally, one evenin', as snowflakes began to fall very delicately, portending the coming blanket of frozen doom, Vance said uneasily, "Raney, I think it's time to go. We doan wanta be caught up in these mountains when the heavy snows come. I think we got ta light out."

Vance was smokin' a pipe, and he puffed away as he said it, fiddlin' with the tobacco in his pocket, taking the pipe out of his mouth, looking at the embers, actin' like he was considerin' whether to add more or leave it be.

He stuck the pipe back in his mouth, and with gritted teeth said, "Time to go, Raney. I'm takin' my bank and lightin' out tomorrow. You can do what you want. I'll leave ya what's left of the provisions." Vance felt relieved, now that he'd spit it out. He looked down, then looked at his pipe, not wanting to confront Raney at all, but not wanting to lie like he did last time.

He knowed he'd done wrong the last time, and he kinda wanted to prove to his pal that he'd become trustworthy again, as if he ever was in the first place.

"You kin go. Good luck to yers." Raney was good with that. He knew Vance didn't know where his Bank was, because what Vance didn't know was that Raney wore his gold sewn into his clothes and his saddle blanket and in his bed pack. Vance had no idea where Raney's Bank was. But Raney knew where Vance's was, because Vance had made a show of lettin' Raney know, not because he was stupid, but because he was stupid-smart. He wanted to regain Raney's trust, because he knowed he'd always need family like Raney. Vance Gann needed someone as knowed his faults and still put up with his mess. Vance knowed it more now as a grown man than he'd done as a younger fella. Raney had been the one all these years who'd been there, and he knowed he had to make it up to Raney as best 'e could.

But Raney wasn't havin' it, because when Raney had first realized, as he started that fatal ponderin' during that smoke, when he'd seed that The Bank had been plundered and knowed he's been screwed again by his childhood pal, Raney was done.

Vance didn't know Raney was done, but Raney was done. And when Vance came back, he'd no idea Raney was done.

Nor did he know that now, as he smoked his corn cob pipe and sighed a breath of release, now that he'd told Raney he was leavin'. Raney said nothing more.

"N' I promise I'm leavin' the provisions, Raney. I won't stiff ya this time." This was the nearest Vance'd ever gotten to admittin' that he's taken the whole kit 'n' caboodle last time. He kinda slipped in that respect; he was so relieved that Raney wasn't angry.

Morning came, and the dawn was chill, and Raney had beat Vance to the punch. He was tendin' the fire and had made some of that thick soup o' coffee and some eggs 'n' beans. Vance was touched that Raney had made 'im a goin' away breakfast of sorts.

"Thanks, Raney," he said, real grateful-like. Raney only nodded in reply. When breakfast was done, Vance got up and adjusted his horse and saddlebags, his bedroll and bags, and at last he went to get his Bank. He rolled away the same old boulder to pull out his own bag of gold. Vance tucked it into the saddlebag and turned to Raney to say good-bye, feelin' a bit misty.

"Lemme show ya what I been doin' before ya go," said Raney, the longest sentence he'd offered Vance in a blue moon. "I wancha to know about this if'n for any reason anything happens."

"Sure, Raney, I'd like to know."

Truth be told, Vance had been dyin' to know, but since Raney'd shut up like a clamshell, Vance'd knowed he'd better just let 'im alone, jest let 'em alone.

Vance followed Raney up the trail and then off into the woods, making footprints in the snow as they went, crunching leaves and branches. They found themselves at a long deep trough in the woods where Raney had been diggin'. "I jest don't get this, Raney. What did you find here?" Vance leaned in to look, and Raney stepped away and back.

"It's my Bank, Vance."

"What?" Vance turned around to look at his friend, who he saw standing there with a six-shootin' equalizer in his hand. Vance's eyes went wide. "What?"

"It's my bank vault, Vance, and I'm about to seal you up in it."

Before Vance could say, "What, Raney, wait!" Raney fired all six shots into his friend's heart, and Vance fell backward into the hole.

Raney went and scraped the snow where some of the blood was into the hole too. Where at other funerals, folks'd throw flowers, clumps of red snow covered his former friend.

Raney quickly got a shovel and began to pour dirt on top of Vance's still warm body, snow steaming up, Vance's glassy eyes still wide with surprise, just like he'd always done, lookin' all innocent-like.

When the deed was done, Raney covered the grave with leaves and branches and other brush and said a prayer for more snow. Then he took his hat off, and looked down, and said, "Sorry, Vance. But you fooled us all oncet too many times. I had to put the quay-bosh on ya. Ya robbed our Bank, brother, and bank robbers usually hang."

On his way back to camp, Raney made sure he'd scooted and scuffled the snow to hide the footsteps of two men. He cleaned the campsite up and burned Vance's bedroll and clothes and set his horse free. He put Vance's bank in his own saddlebag, and then, before he decided to take off for Denver, he sat down, rolled hisself a big fat quirley, and blew smoke rings into the cold crisp air.

CAROL GIMBEL

THE GUARDIAN

Carol Gimbel, former cooking columnist for the Oklahoma City *Tribune* for eight years and a radio host for KRPT-radio, is a frequent contributor to *Guideposts* magazine. Author of the novel *Raven's Song*, she now resides in Oklahoma City with her husband Woody and two dogs.

THE GUARDIAN

by Carol Gimbel

Perched high in the top of a cottonwood, a hawk watched and waited.

Crouched in a blackberry thicket, thorns tearing at his arms, a man spat in the sand and idly watched an ant trudge through the mud he'd just made. He wiped his mouth with the back of his hand and tried not to think about the dull pounding behind his eyes.

"She thinks she can just waltz back here after all this time and take my land," he grumbled. "Hope she's enjoying this day. It's gonna be her last."

Sun warmed the barrel of the rifle lying across his knee. He picked it up, closed one eye, and looked through the scope. The smoothness of the stock against his cheek comforted him, familiar as an old friend. He swung the barrel down toward the spot where the trail emerged from the trees. His eyes narrowed as he detected movement in the shadows. He waited, his finger curved almost lovingly around the trigger.

Nothing. Was his imagination playing tricks on him

again?

Slowly, almost imperceptibly, his finger tightened. Sweat trickled into his eyes, stinging like hell and blurring his vision. He blinked. Time stopped and held its breath along with him.

A doe moved cautiously from the grove of trees. With one quick sweep, she surveyed the canyon floor. Then, as if aware that the crosshairs of his scope met across her heart, she raised her head and looked directly at the man crouched on the ledge. The doe regarded him with large liquid eyes. For endless seconds, he wrestled with the temptation to squeeze the trigger, to take her life, just because he could.

The doe stood perfectly still, nothing moving but her ears. Then, deciding the man didn't present a threat today, she looked over her shoulder. A fawn wearing a camouflage coat pranced out of the shadows to scamper beside his mother as she picked her way down the trail.

He lowered the gun, laid it back across his knee, and waited.

ෆ౭

"You seem to be in a big hurry to get wherever you're going," the girl told her horse. "But I'm not, so cool it." At the canyon's edge she reined in.

The view from there was spectacular. All her senses feasted on her surroundings, like a death row inmate downing his last meal. She savored the scent of the horse beneath her, the earth, cedar, and fresh air. Her eyes devoured the sights, a profusion of extravagantly colored wildflowers dancing in the distance and the clear blue of the sky above. Trees were a mosaic of green in the canyon below. She breathed in deeply and raised her face to the sky, enjoying the sun's warmth and the kiss of the southern breeze. A mockingbird somewhere behind her trilled through his repertoire. His song and the jingle of the bridle as the horse mouthed the bit were the only sounds to be heard.

Her soul had cried out to be someplace where she could breathe. The serenity of this land was far from the noise and traffic of the city from which she'd escaped. But now the city was just a tangle of memories.

She felt a twinge of guilt that her grandmother had left this land to her instead of her cousin Fred, as everyone had expected, but not enough to spoil this perfect day.

She would bask in the glorious peace and perfection the day offered her. Never had she felt so at home. She belonged here to this land, and this land belonged to her. And after a lifetime of searching, of feeling that she never quite fit into her own life, the knowledge was intoxicating.

She guided the little mare down the narrow trail to the canyon floor. The trail snaked along the canyon wall and through a grove of trees.

As she neared the edge of the woods, the cry of a hawk broke the silence. She looked up. The hawk watched from the top of a giant cottonwood and shrieked again. He seemed to want something from her, but the girl had no idea what. She reined in and looked up at him. Unblinking, he looked back.

As she urged her horse forward and emerged from the woods, the shriek of the hawk pierced the silence. The hawk dove from its lofty perch into a blackberry thicket. A gunshot echoed through the canyon.

"Strange," she muttered. "Who would have fireworks out here?" She stopped to listen again. She heard a garbled scream and something crashing through the underbrush. Then it was gone, and all was silent again.

The hawk swooped low and flew ahead of her to the top of a cottonwood on down the trail. The hawk was too far away for the girl to see the blood on his talons.

"What a glorious day to be alive!" She said the words out loud, although there was no one around to hear her but the horse. And the hawk.

The hawk watched and waited.

WOODY GIMBEL

THE KEEPER OF THE GATE

Woody Gimbel has written book reviews and articles on leadership, psychology, and religion. A fan of books by Louis L'Amour and Tony Hillerman, as well as the Western movies by John Ford and Henry Hawks, he has loved the Western Genre since early childhood. He is currently working on an epic futuristic sci-fi series that finds a world-governing, highly-evolved, self-aware Artificial Intelligence stymied by self-doubt and deep questions about its own less-than-human algorithms. Woody and his wife live in Warr Acres, OK, with their two rescue dogs Geisha and Annie.

THE KEEPER OF THE GATE

by Woody Gimbel

The old man slept, head resting on a pillow fashioned of desert sand. Cool early morning air stirred. Alerted senses awakened to darkness as night sounds withdrew into silence, yielding to approaching day life. The old man stood and faced east, speaking words of the Navajo Sing he was teaching the boy.

"Wake up and listen, for your time is near," he said.

The boy rubbed the sleep from his eyes, emerging slowly from his blanket. He was in no hurry, but he was glad to be here with the old man, to learn his ways, and to preserve the Sing.

"Yes, Teacher! I am ready to listen," the boy said. "Is your time always so early and dark?" The old man laughed. He understood the boy. The boy spoke in three levels.

"Yes, for me the time is always so early and dark. Why do you ask?"

The boy answered respectfully, "Teacher, you have taught me that it must be so for you. But must it be both so early and so dark for me at my time?"

"My Student, you will learn if you do not already know. Through darkness, we see more clearly, more deeply, into the secrets of creation, life, and death. The three worlds beneath this world."

In his mind the old man heard the thunder that announced the beginning of creation, echoing from that ancient moment to be heard at the beginning of each day. Each day is the recreation of the world, from darkness into light, death to life, from sleep to alertness and action for living things in this world.

"Listen, boy. Listen closely. Your time is soon," the old man whispered. Filled with awe and joy, the old man began to walk within a circle symbolizing the abode of the Great Spirit. Stamping his feet in time with the cadence of the sing, he high-stepped with the agility and energy of a young man.

For creation we thank you Great Spirit. From darkness you made light.

You open the Day Gate slowly. You prepare us for the light.

Night dies birthing Sun Child. How many deaths, how many births?

Sun Child arrows ignite Fire Cloud, Fire Cloud proclaims a new creation,

Sun Child will grow stronger, to warm the dine'e and yes, the belagana, too.

Mountain Lion, Coyote, Crow, and Hummingbird, awaken. Men, arise, dine'e, and yes, belagana, too.

From the sacred to the sacred, you survey this world from East to West.

Growing our corn and squash and gourds, Providing children, and offspring to all,

Feeding our families and filling our streams. Until Old Sun retires from this day's work,

Until darkness returns, when all will rest, another creation will surely follow.

The boy, trembling with inexpressible joy, said, "Teacher, I hear your words. I preserve them in my heart. With this Sing I am prepared for my time."

"Yes, boy, you have listened well. We must be about our day's work. Bring my pony."

"Why do we go? Why are the belegana as they are?"

"Boy, it is because the belegana are troubled with

the Spirit Sickness. We cannot cure them. They do not hunger for harmony. But we must do what is necessary. Spirit Sickness makes them crazy. You will see. We will do what is necessary. We will prepare the way for our spirits, and the spirits of our ancestors to prevail in this time of the belegana. To be ready when the Great Spirit restores harmony to this world."

"I hear and revere your words, Teacher, but I do not understand their meaning. Still, I will do as you say, for you are my Teacher."

"Teacher, I will bring your pony," the boy said softly.

☙❧

The old man eased himself forward on the calm pinto and accepted the reins from the boy. The boy mounted his spirited chestnut with a lightning-streak blaze. Blaze snorted his impatience to start the journey. The boy reined Blaze in, following Pinto.

The scream of a hawk far overhead marked the descent of a hungry hunter to seize an unwary desert mammal. The belegana were like that hawk in one respect—preying on the unwary, but unlike the hawk in another respect—the hawk kills to survive. The belegana just kill and destroy. Although the boy could not see the capture, he heard the small animal shriek, joined by a chorus of protesting relatives. The hawk snatched its unwilling meal and carried it aloft to a dining place, perhaps to feed its fledglings. The cries against the injustice of it all faded into the desert as Pinto and Blaze plodded toward town.

"Such is life," the old man had taught the boy. "Hawks live in harmony as the Great Spirit willed. Belegana live like belegana, not in harmony, predators without purpose. The Great Spirit tells us this race escaped from the third underworld before their time. They stole their way to the upper world. The upper world has suffered ever since. There is hope," the old man said solemnly, "regardless of the evil that invaded, not all belegana are belegana!" The boy believed but did not understand.

The old man and the boy rode into town.

A rough belegana shouted, "Look, that there's the half-breed. What do you see in him, old man? We got no use for his kind."

The preacher's wife shouted loudly, "You know

why the boy's here. You're the heathen, not the boy." She wanted everyone to know where she stood. As the old man had said, "Not all belegana are belegana."

Heathen glared at preacher's wife. All eyes focused on him. He backed down, said nothing, made his way to the Saloon.

The old man and the boy dismounted, tied up their ponies. Hand on the boy's shoulder, the old man entered Fancie's Fine Saloon with the boy. It was fine in its time. When Fancie left Twin Gulch eighteen years ago, she took the "fine" with her. The saloon deteriorated into weekend drunken brawls, shootings, and gambling. No place for dine'e. On week days, the saloon served as courtroom, town hall, telegraph office, and unoccupied sheriff's office—no one wore the badge since Fancie left.

"Order in the court," shouted the bailiff. "The court is now in session, His Honor Ashton Blake presiding. All rise." Everyone stood as the judge took the bench.

The old man approached the bar serving as the judge's bench and said, "We are here."

The boy had heard the angry words leading to the fight. He alone witnessed the killing. Standing in shadow between the saloon and the livery stable, unseen by the combatants, he had repeated the words leading up to the fatal shooting. The boy had no gun, no motive, no violent tendency. The accused had drunk heavily with the shooting victim before the fight broke out.

The boy was here to answer the judge's questions. Problem was he only told what he heard. People thought the boy strange but never considered him capable of killing. Other than the hatred of narrow-minded townspeople, no one had anything against the boy.

Jared Higgins, the accused, sat handcuffed beside the bailiff. When the boy approached the bench, the judge glanced up at the accused. Higgins began to chant, "The injun boy done it! He done it! The half-breed done it!" Louder and louder. No order in the court.

"The half breed done it!" Higgins' drinking buddies joined in.

Everyone in the courtroom was astonished when the judge stated, "Boy. You are under arrest for suspicion of killin' Wesley Banks at 9:30 on the evening of April 18. Bailiff, take him into custody. Release Higgins. He's free to go."

The courtroom erupted in anger.

The judge explained his decision. "We thought

about what you said about the shootin'. You was right there, for sure. But it don't add up. You ain't tellin' us what you seen, what they was wearin' an all. Don't make sense. Nobody remembers word for word like 'less they made it up. You ain't blind, but you didn't see nothing. Why did you do it?"

The boy had no legal representation. The old man approached the boy. The judge didn't object. Assuming the role of defense, the old man said, "My boy, tell us what you know."

The boy recited again what he had heard, word for word, perfectly duplicating each voice.

"You pay me what you owe me, you scoundrel!" The boy captured Higgins' intonation perfectly.

"Hail, no! You cheated me, an' I just took back what's mine." Perfect imitation of Wesley Banks.

"No way. Give me my money. That'll settle it. You done me wrong." Jared Higgins' voice.

"If you ain't givin' it to me, I'll just take it," Wesley Banks' voice.

"I'm drawin' my gun now. Don't make me use it." Jared Higgins' voice.

"Put down that gun, Jared." Wesley Banks' voice.

"You asked for it." Jared Higgins' voice.

"Damn. You done shot me." Wesley Banks' voice.

"What you lookin' at, injun?" Jared Higgins' voice.

"Your honor, that's what he knows. He is not guilty. The boy does not lie," the old man said.

The people in the courtroom murmured agreement. They wanted justice. Even if Higgins *might not* be guilty, the boy was certainly innocent.

Judge Blake stood, banged his gavel a final time and said, "The verdict is guilty. Take the boy away, bailiff. He will be hanged at sunset."

The court erupted, shouting their disagreement to the judge who walked off unaffected.

The old man put one hand on the boy's lips, handed him a small pellet from his pouch with the other hand.

The boy understood. He accepted the pellet, put it in his mouth, and smiled.

The townspeople in the courtroom vented their wrath on Jared Higgins. "Higgins, how can you let another one die? You heathen! It's your kind we don't want. Speak up for this boy."

"You injun lovers! You heard the judge. I'm free. The boy's gonna hang. It's the law," Higgins said.

The shouting subsided when the boy slumped in a lifeless heap onto the floor. The doctor pushed through the people to the boy's side. He checked for pulse, breathing, any sign of life. "This boy flat out died. There won't be any hanging this evening."

Higgins gloated above the din, "Proves he's guilty."

The old man turned in the direction of Higgins' voice. He pronounced an ancient truth curse on Higgins.

Not knowing why, Higgins burst loudly into a complete confession. "I done it. I killed Wesley, just like the injun boy said. I'm the one. I'm guilty. The boy's innnocent."

The bailiff brought the judge back into the courtroom to hear Higgins still proclaiming his guilt. The judge, red-faced, proclaimed "The previous verdict was premature. In the light of new evidence, the boy is innocent. Higgins is guilty. I sentence him to hanging at sunset. Bailiff, arrest him and take him to his cell."

ଌଃ଼ଠ

At sunset, the bailiff brought Higgins to the customary gallows tree. He was hung by the neck, pronounced dead by the doctor. The crowd watched in silence, sobered by the death of the innocent boy.

The undertaker brought two wooden caskets. Higgins and the boy were placed inside, lids tacked on, and loaded on the wagon that would take them to the town cemetery. The undertaker tied Pinto and Blaze to the back of the wagon, helped the old man into the seat. They started up the hill.

As the wagon reached the crest, the old man smiled to himself. The boy's time had come. Earlier than hoped.

The undertaker stopped the wagon at the gate, helped the old man down. He slid the caskets down the tailgate onto the sandy ground.

"This is where I turn 'em over to you, Ancient One," the undertaker spoke with reverence. He and the old man shared a belief in a justice beyond death. This comforted the undertaker. He knew the two caskets were headed on different journeys.

"For fifty years, you've sent them on their final journey. The Keeper of the Gate. I can remember when you were established, so long ago. I saw you take the pellet from your Teacher. You died for all to see. The next thing we knew, you were alive, back here at this gate, and your Teacher was gone. Wasn't that long ago your eyes could see, like the rest of us see. Now you see in ways we can't."

"Your daughter was beaten by the same white man who got her pregnant. Desert Flower, we called her. Miss Fancie tried to save her. They beat her near to death. Then, that man's people beat you and the sheriff. Deputies betrayed him and gouged your eyes out.

"She was carrying the boy, your grandson. He almost died. Might be why he's the way he is. She died giving birth. When those bastards went free, Miss Fancie couldn't live in a town like this. She went back home in the East. We never heard from her again. You stayed. Keeper of the Gate."

The Ancient One spoke: "Mr. Wells, you told the story rightly. You who saw me established. You gave me the pellet when my daughter was killed, after I was blinded. You gave the potion that brought me back. The men thought I was dead. They left me alone. They killed the sheriff. Now, you can see my grandson established, Desert Rain. Open his casket, please."

Mr. Wells extracted the nails, and removed the casket cover. The old man and the undertaker gazed on the boy lying peacefully. The old man administered the potion, gently opening the boy's mouth, and placing it under his tongue. In moments, the boy stirred, opened one eye, then the other. He smiled, sat up, and asked,

"Where am I?"

"My grandson, you are home. You will be established. The undertaker, Mr. Wells will return to town. The people will come to see you. They will know you are the rightful Keeper of the Gate. Tell them that you have come home, and your grandfather has gone home."

"Grandfather, how will I get along without you? I hear, but I cannot see with these eyes, while you see without eyes. My understanding is shallow."

"You will be established. For the first time, you will see and hear with understanding. At birth, you received gifts to sustain you until you could be established. Your gift was memory for the Sing. Now you will have all the gifts of the Keeper of the Gate."

The undertaker returned to town. The boy and the old man moved Higgins' casket onto a cart and wheeled it to the cemetery. They slid the casket through the door to the underworld.

The old man began his walk to the upper world, relieved of the duties in this world.

Desert Rain began the Evening Sing. When people see him, they will know he is Keeper of the Gate.

JOHNNA KAYE

MUDDY AS BLACK AND WHITE

Johnna Kaye is a graduate of the University of Oklahoma, where she earned her master's degree in French literature. Before starting her family, she spent a year living in France and ten years teaching French in the United States. Author of *Token* and *Viral* of *The Casdan Chronicles* series, Kaye resides in Central Oklahoma with a devoted husband, two teenage children, two cats, and one very pesky dog.

MUDDY AS BLACK AND WHITE

by Johnna Kaye

"Take it back, Billy!" She shoved the boy in the chest, and he fell flat in the mud. It was quite a feat for a scrawny girl half his size, but not if you knew Josie. She didn't take comments like that from bullies, even when they weren't exactly about her.

"You know it's true, Jo-se-phin-a!"

"No, it's not! And it's Josie!" She kicked her foot out as hard as she could, but he caught it and twisted. Josie fell over him and proceeded to pummel his chest and everything else that got in the way.

The school kids encircled them and began chanting their names.

"Come on, Jo!"

"Don't let a girl beat you up, Billy!"

Mrs. Lamb trotted out. "Back inside, children! All of you!" She tugged their shoulders, nudging them toward the school. She'd been wondering where her class had gone. They should've been back from lunch by now. "Go on!" She waved her arms as she neared the tangle of limbs.

"Josie! What's got into you?" She dragged the nine-year old up to her feet and wiped at the mud on her face with her apron.

"He started it!" Josephina pointed accusingly at Billy. He sat up and wiped at the mud on his arms.

"Did not!"

"Did too!"

"Stop it right now! Both of you!" Mrs. Lamb took a good long look at Billy. He appeared none the worse for wear except for a spot of blood on his lip—and the mud. She sighed.

The natural question should've been "What happened?" But she didn't have to ask. She'd been wondering how long it'd take before she and her husband would have to move from their newest home. The way Billy had been watching her and Mr. White…

"All right, Billy. Go home and get cleaned up. I'll talk to your Pa after school."

"He don't want to talk to you!"

"I'll be here, anyway. Now, go on. Tell him I'll be here after school if he wants to see me."

Mrs. Lamb held out her hand, but Billy's sour face looked her up and down in a demonstration of disgust.

He rolled over the other way, lumbered to his feet, and trudged off toward home.

Mrs. Lamb and Josephina watched until he was out of earshot. "Do you care to tell me what that was all about?"

Lips puckered, Josie looked down at her feet and shook her head.

"I didn't think so." Mrs. Lamb tilted Josephina's chin up until their eyes connected. "Looks like you got the better of Billy."

"Yes, Ma'am." Josie's eyes twinkled with a pride she couldn't voice to Mrs. Lamb.

Mrs. Lamb snickered. "Come on, then." She led Josie by the shoulder back to the one-room building. As she reached the door, the other kids scampered across the wood floor to their seats. Josie walked head-down to her desk, fully aware everyone was watching her. She wiped her nose with the back of her hand and sat down.

The help, Mr. White, put more wood in the stove. He exchanged a sidelong glance with Mrs. Lamb that said they needed to talk, but not right then and there.

"All right, children. It's time for arithmetic."

The kids moaned and creaked open their desktops

for their chalk-boards.

※

"Are you sure?" Mrs. Lamb asked that evening as she handed her husband a bowl of hot stew.

"There's little doubt in my mind, Sarah. Billy must've heard about us."

"But we've been so careful this time. Other than the schoolhouse, I don't even walk through town if you're there."

"I don't know how they figured it out, but I'm certain they did. Oh, my sweet Sarah. I'm no good for you. Nothing good can come from us," he lamented.

"How can you say that? You're the most respectful, kindest, most gentle man I've ever known. You have far more dignity than those backward townsfolk ever had. I'm never leaving you, so just put that outta' your head, you hear?"

Les rubbed his calloused hand over his short curly hair. He let out a tremendous sigh. "We'll never have a proper wedding, you know that. No judge will marry a white woman to a man of color. We'll have to keep livin' in sin."

"We've been through this. Common-law marriage is perfectly legal."

"Townsfolk tend to disagree."

"Well, I don't care what they say! I love you, and that's that! We'll just move again if we have to!" Sarah squeezed into his lap with an ornery smile. He pushed his chair back from the table and wrapped his hands around her. He couldn't help smiling. She always did that to him. He couldn't say no to her, no matter how hard he tried.

She took his face in her hands and looked him square-on. "I love you, Leslie White, and that's my final word." She proceeded to kiss him in a way that proved her point and ended the conversation.

☙❧

An early-morning knock at the door startled Sarah. She didn't think anyone knew where they lived; they were so far out in the woods. She opened it to find one of her students staring up at her.

"Good morning, Mrs. Lamb." He handed her a note. "The sheriff asked me to bring you this."

"Why, thank you, Micah…"

The boy ran off before she could say anything more. She closed the door and opened the letter.

"What's it say?" Les crawled out of the armoire in the corner. He peered over her shoulder to read along.

"My *presence* is *requested*," she spat the words. Les pulled a bag out of the armoire and began stuffing their belongings inside. Sarah pulled her Sunday dress out of his hands.

"Now, hold on. Let me go talk to him. Maybe it's not about us. Maybe it's about Billy, or… or maybe it's the supplies I requested earlier this week."

Les stepped around her and continued to find the most important belongings to take with them. He pulled his pistol out of the drawer and stuffed it in the back of his breeches.

"Just what do you think you're doin'?" Sarah gaped. She followed him as he continued his search for things to pack.

"Sarah…" He stopped for a moment to look her in the eye. "Nothin' good can come from this meetin'. You know how this will end. Same as the last two. I'm getting you outta' here, right now."

"You're just assuming this is about us! Maybe—"

"You know it is!"

"We don't!" Sarah stood defiant, willing him to listen. He walked around her again, this time out the door. She followed him around back where he pulled off the rocks hiding the buried cache of valuables. "Leslie White! You listen to me!"

"No!" He stood and grabbed onto her forearms. His strength surprised her. He was normally so gentle with her. "You listen to me! We're leaving! Now, go get your things!" He let go and went back to unburying their cache. Sarah stamped her foot once then turned on her heel. She ran to the lean-to and bridled their horse. She hopped on and galloped away bareback like she used to when she was a little girl.

"Sarah!" Leslie called desperately after her.
It was too late. She rounded the bend, heading into town.

൙൏

Sarah arrived winded, but resolute. She slid off the old appaloosa and tied him to the post. She took a deep breath and tried in vain to tame her wild hair. She braided it and left it to dangle loosely down her back. At least, she was dressed for the day.

As she climbed the steps, the clomp of spurs and boots against the floor inside announced the sheriff's presence. He opened the door and motioned her in.

"Mrs. Lamb."

"You wanted to see me?" Sarah held her chin high and confident. "If this is about the supplies I requisitioned—"

"This ain't about the supplies."

"No?" Her voice was too high for her own liking. She cleared her throat and lifted her chin again, pulling her shoulders back stiffer than they already were.

"Nooo." He chuckled as if scolding a child. "This is about your loose morals, Mrs. Lamb. Or should I say… Mrs. White."

"Why, I don't know what you're talking about! Mr. White is my—"

"Mr. White isn't just your help. You've broken the law."

Sarah stood abruptly. "I've broken no laws, Sheriff. I will not stand here and listen to you—"

"I've got 'im, Sheriff!" a voice called from outside. Sarah's eyes flew to the window where she saw Leslie, his hands tied behind his back. He'd been beaten, and one eye was already swelling shut. She raced out the door.

"Leslie!" She let out a blood-curdling scream and ran to him. She took his swollen face in her hands and took in every painful detail. This time looked to be worse than the last. They'd threatened to whip him before, but she'd managed to talk them out of it with a promise to leave him and the town before it'd come to that.

"I'm sorry, Miss," Les lied. "I'll give back everything I took. You don't have to worry 'bout me no more. I'll leave town. You'll never have to see me again."

Sarah stood firm next to him and faced her accusers. "I will not stand for this! Release this man, right this instant! He's my—"

The sheriff chuckled. "Oh, we know right well what he is to you."

A man walked out of the sheriff's building. She'd noticed little noises from a room in back, but assumed it'd been prisoners in their cell, perhaps a deputy.

"Howdy do, Mrs. White."

"M… Mr. Halsey," Sarah stammered at seeing the deputy from Sparrow Brook. He'd personally escorted her and Les out of that town. "Whatever are you doing here?"

"Just following up on a rumor."

"I don't see how it's any business of yours!"

"It's everyone's business! Isn't that right?" the sheriff yelled. He gestured around them. A crowd had begun to gather on the sidewalks and doors. A few men hooted in support of the sheriff.

Sarah's head pivoted, taking in the faces staring back at them with disdain.

"Stop it! Ya'll hear?" A young voice cried out. Sarah's heart stopped for a moment. The voice was unmistakable. *No,* she silently implored. She swallowed her nausea. She was willing to do what it took to free Leslie, but she also loved her school kids. She couldn't bear to see any of them involved in her affairs.

"Let him go!" Josie screamed, her voice cracking at the end. She rode in on a horse. Everyone squinted her way to find she wasn't alone. Behind her, five other horses arrived.

She jumped off her horse, and the black man behind her slid off struggling to keep up with her as she ran into Sarah's arms. An awkward shuffle ensued as if both were trying to protect the other. Josie faced the sheriff. "They ain't done nothin' wrong!"

"Run along, child. This is no business of yours." The sheriff looked put out with the distraction.

"Is too! If you hurt them, you have to hurt all of us!" Josie insisted.

"Josie, what are you doin'? Run along before it's too late! This is no place for you!" Sarah tried to speak calmly to her, but it came out in a rush.

"It is, too, my place. And his and all theirs…" She pointed to the men and women walking up to join them, whites, colored people… even a Mexican woman. "It's time for change around here! This here's my Pa! He raised me!" Sarah met the eyes of the black man, whose hands rested protectively on Josie's shoulders. A small grin was exchanged between them, and they all turned in solidarity to face the sheriff.

"And Billy's ma's an Indian!" Sarah followed Josie's eyes to Billy.

His face disappeared behind the post of the saloon before he took off running into the woods behind it.

The click of a gun alerted everyone's attention back to the sheriff, then to the deputy across the street. Their guns were now drawn and pointed at them.

The air around them shifted, and the womenfolk

began hustling the children inside the buildings, their heads peering out the windows to watch.

Sarah turned beseechingly to the folks around her. "Surely you don't all agree with the sheriff here, do you? Why, I'm an educated woman! I'm your schoolmaster, for pity's sake! Just ask any of your children as to the character of either of us…"

More guns were raising to point at them from all sides. Clicks of triggers being cocked announced that the townfolk were casting their votes.

The black woman standing a yard away tapped a bulge on her thigh, and Sarah knew; they'd all come prepared. She swallowed and nodded ever so slightly to Josie's dad, then threw herself onto Les in a dramatic display. She wrapped her arms around him, feigning the damsel in distress the crowd all wanted to see.
Her hand reached under the back of his vest and found the gun. She wrapped her fingers firmly around it. She shoved Leslie to the ground and fired the first shot.

Gunfire erupted all around her. Mr. Halsey went down first. She made sure of that. She saw the deputy go down too but wasn't sure if he was dead or not. After that, it was all a blur of gun-powdered smoke, blood, and ear-splitting chaos. Leslie bled freely from the chest, and little Josie lay on the ground lifeless as a doll.

Sarah's gun clicked, emptied of bullets. She'd been wounded but didn't care. She searched the dead bodies around her for another gun, desperate to finish the job.
Then, everything went silent. Her heart thumped wildly in her chest and mingled with the ringing in her ears. The sheriff's spurs clinked closer and closer, and a strange calmness came over her. She dropped her gun and watched him narrow the distance.

Senses numbed, she turned a tempestuous circle looking at the people walking out, staring, and watching her. She laughed contemptuously. "Is this what you wanted? Look what you've done!" She gestured wildly to indicate the friends at her feet.

The sheriff fired one last time.

଒ଃ଼

There was a funeral of sorts the next day. The townsfolk all came out to help dig the mass grave. The bodies were all piled in together, and the dirt was thrown in on top. Words were said.

"…in care of our children, no less."

"… living in sin like that…"

The sheriff hammered in a sign in front of the raised mound. He read the words at the top of the sign, so the illiterate townsfolk would know, "Justice was served."

BERNADETTE LOWE

THE ORPHAN TRAIN

Bernadette Lowe grew up on a dairy farm and lived with a wolf who taught her respect. She is now a grandmother who loves writing stories for her granddaughter and lives in Oklahoma City, OK.

THE ORPHAN TRAIN TRANSPORTING 250,000 HOMELESS CHILDREN TO BE GIVEN AWAY TO STRANGERS

by Bernadette Lowe

Picture the USA around 1900 in your mind: Huge ships docked everywhere with a thousand new immigrants daily overfilling a big city. Epidemics coming and going with multitudes of people buried six foot under, leaving children homeless, needy, with no one to care for them.

Left to fend for themselves, children dirty, dressed in rags, sleeping in alleys, sheds, and streets. A starving brother would steal food for his little sister and find himself, age five, in adult jail. Separated from her only known living family, his sister would wander, dirty, hungry, tired, all alone, crying, with no help in sight.

She wouldn't even know her last name. Rats were everywhere, the stench unbearable, and mud from the streets would fill her little shoes and seep inside, wetting her cold feet. She, like thousands of children, was homeless, running rampant, filling overcrowded streets.

Over 10,000 homeless children slept on streets in New York City, alone. This was America.

Life could be harsh. Times were hard and there was no money. Men rode horses, carried guns, and bread was earned with the sweat of the brow. Pride determined that each and every person earned their way.

Medical attention was minimal and doctors were paid in chickens, meat, and grain. A black bag was sufficient to carry all that was needed to diagnose a disease, to remove a bullet, to suture a wound, or to save a life. Bought groceries were limited to salt, pepper, sugar, and possibly flour. All else was bartered or grown at home.

We were an agriculture-based nation and people lived on farms consisting of hundreds of acres. Many chopped cotton and hoed crops as whirlwinds tossed over barren soil.

Work was done by hand, because reapers or binders were rare. Walking plows and sulky plows were like a few minuscule drops of paint on the landscape. Small towns existed, and tiny remnants of the great Indian civilization still spurred rare raids. Homes had shotguns; windows and doors were open and unlocked. Food was hard to come by, and another mouth to feed was one too many.

In New York City, there were no jobs, and parents watched as their young cried and fell asleep with growling, hungry bellies. Their bodies had sunken bones that showed through their clothes.

Many parents could not afford the children, much less themselves. In desperation, parents sent older children to the streets to steal food, to sleep, just to survive. Many babies were placed in bassinets that sat outside the almshouse with a note attached, stating the name and a hope to return for the child. With broken hearts and tears in their eyes, they walked away from their own children, never to see them again.

Add to this all the homeless children whose parents died from TB, the flu, yellow fever, etc., or whose parents abandoned bad children.

Others were sent to jail or were forced to return to the motherland, leaving behind their young, and the children caught pilfering.

Children were taken away, because parents were poor, or their morality was in question. Thus, thousands of children lived on the streets, alone, in every large city, with not one soul in charge.

Dying parents, in multitudes, begged someone to take in their children. Homeless children were of epidemic proportions.

At the insistence of Charles Brace, many of these children were farmed out to rural farmers, sweatshops, and factories. Contracts required a home, hard work, schooling, and spiritual guidance in hopes of introducing morality. Some were paid wages.

Churches mentioned the plight of the orphans on Sundays. Courthouse steps across the nation posted their next arrival. Newspapers made sure the community was aware of the exact day to receive a child. In town and on farms, everyone knew homeless children were offered. This distribution system was a well oiled machine in the business of placing out children to strangers.

A young child was considered capable of making decisions and working. For those, age six and older, it took receipt of a small letter applying for a child and a nod from several members of the community to receive a warm-bodied laborer to work fields and harvest crops.

A paid western agent had already initiated a selection committee usually consisting of the sheriff, pastor, newspaper editor, banker, and/or owner of the general store who had the task to find good potential families.

This mail order list was provided to the Children's Aid Society to use in selecting children based on sex, age, color of hair and eyes. There were over 600 orphanages with 50,000 homeless waifs at this time.

In turn, farmers signed certificates to keep them till age 21, clothe them, feed them, send them to school for a few months a year, and to attend church. Children were on trial for 30 days and could be removed. They arrived in cattle cars on the railroad to serve the workforce of the family who requested them.

For some, their future was being overworked, malnourished, and even mistreated. Yet, it was the best option available to save their lives.

Many found good homes and loving people. These little children came on the Orphan Train and were the last remnant of mass indentured servants in America.

The Foundling Home, run by Catholic nuns, matched babies to families with the help of Catholic priests. These trains were called the Baby Train and/or the Mercy Train. Older children, regardless of religion, were put on the Orphan Train to Catholic homes and expected to learn a new language, if needed. Most of these children were adopted, and a checkup was performed one time.

The little neglected street urchins were held from days to weeks in asylums, and orphanages, waiting for the next monthly train departure. The destitute vagrants were gathered, advertised, and no different than cattle, put in boxcars on trains to be distributed. Some cars had the stench of vomit and feces, making it difficult to bed children. Each child rode the rails, searching for new kin, a name, a home, and most received work in return. Such was the Orphan Train.

Placing a little note that had a number and a name on their clothing, they were loaded in train cars and escorted by nuns, nurses, or western agents.

The little number would match a prospective farmer or parent who would meet them at the stops. The trains carried anywhere from a few children up to 300 per train monthly with additional trips in spring and summer when laborers were needed.

Arriving at every station, their caretakers gave them a bible, a bath, changed their clothes, putting the dirty set in their little cardboard suitcase which held all their belongings, possibly a family treasure.

Baby boys wore dresses. Girls were given a hair bow. It was a sad procession as they were lined up, tallest to shortest and walked to a waiting meal or stage.

For those not ordered, prospective takers listened as children sang a church song or recited a poem. Children, six and older, had a greater chance of being chosen because of their ability to work. As they were plucked out, they were expected to make a decision on the spot, to go with the stranger or not. Traveling state after state, the train grew lighter as children were shown, measured for strength and durability, or performed sit-ups, sized up and down, spoken to, and selection was made by strangers needing help or wanting a child, possibly unable to bear one of their own.

At times, one spouse would select a child, take him to her home, and surprise the other spouse. Every imaginable situation existed as these children were mail ordered, selected, adopted, received a work contract, or were simply placed. Imagine siblings on the train, hoping to find a home together, reaching a stop along the way. The youngest holds tightly to eldest's leg when they are pried apart, and one is chosen. The other is left behind. Most times, this separation of families became permanent.

At each stop along the way, every child that could be matched was met with an unloading of a burden placed upon the train. The Orphan Train was our first welfare contract, first documented foster care system, and served as a living laboratory.

Each unloading of a passenger was the same. They either went to work or met possible parents, an agreement was reached, and a trip to the county courthouse sealed the deal. Adoption papers were filed, the judge signed off, and each chosen child was at a new home by day's end. Judges did not say no, because welfare left with the Orphan Train.

Some were adopted, as kind people stretched to take them in. Benches, where their own children sat as they ate the meager food that existed, were squeezed tight to hold another warm body, ensuring the work load was easier. Clothing was shared, handed down, and worn carefully as frayed and ragged edges could easily split and tear. Scraps from old worn clothing were precious commodities used to patch and repair frail clothing.

For those adopted into a large family of siblings, some must have felt strange. There, while they did become part of the family, some knew that they were different, an outsider on the inside, but always looking in from the outside. Some children thrived and did well, others felt slighted, but all knew this had been the only option for them. They had no choice over their lives.

In Boston, a barber and his wife died from TB. His sons Fred, age five, and John Haberer, age three, eventually came on the Orphan Train with Catholic nuns to Templetown, Iowa, and found placement. Fred was adopted by Frank and Mary Mosman and took their last name.

John went to live with Mary Mosman's parents, changed his name to John Peter Hoberer, taking Peter Roth's first name and changing the spelling of his last name.

The families spoke German, but Fred and John only spoke English, making it very scary. John moved with Fred and the Mosmans to Kansas and then to Lindsay, Texas where he slept in the back of the Hoelker family grocery store. He was only ten years old but was determined to be near his brother, who was now his uncle.

Every stop at the Gainesville, Texas depot was the same, every month: distribution day for the homeless of the homeless, for this was the last stop.

Each and every child must be found a home.

Two barren couples, each neighbors, had discussed the possibility of finding a child on the Orphan Train. Leo and Katy Mosser never adopted a child. The other couple, the Eges, hooked up horse and carriage and proceeded to town with hopeful hearts for a young boy. Arriving early, they waited, heart in hand. Standing at the depot, which was a large one room building that seemed to stretch and stretch, they stood, pacing the floor, waiting for the child they so desperately wanted and needed.

As the train pulled into the last stop, hope must have almost faded from sight.

The children gathered by the windows, sticking their heads out, eyes showing their plight, their concern, wondering if this would be the day that they would be chosen, receive a name, a home and a mom and dad.

This particular day, a small, thin wisp of a boy appeared. Quiet, with big blue eyes, he was shy and withdrawn, in shock. Looking downward, he waited to be passed over. It was this quietness, this need for love that attracted him to his new parents. The judge did not deny the adoption, for welfare had departed with the train.

At another "dispersement", four small children whose parents had died from the flu had made a promise to their dying parents that they would not be separated. Stop after stop, one or another of the children would be chosen, but not one family would take all four children. These four little kids held hands tightly and refused to be split.

Waiting for the train, families showed and lined up at the depot. The Mosters decided to take Steve and Frank. The Sickings decided to take Teresa and Tony (who had been born in Italy) and promised the children that they would be together every Sunday, God permitting. It was best and the eldest child realized this. There were no more stops. They must be adopted and today.

No other couples were interested in four children. The families, almost strangers, would be at one another's houses every week for half a day, tied together with words of honor.

The Sickings had a farm in Lindsay, Texas. The Mosters added four children of their own, and eventually Steve and Frank moved in with the Sickings. They had never thought it possible to live together again. Steve Moster married and had children.

Frank was killed in service. Teresa and Tony never

married and took care of their parents, very grateful they found a home. Teresa vacationed in every state in the U.S. in a car with no air conditioner and a fan hooked to the cigarette lighter. She loved life.

Ironically, the Eges and Mossers were also neighbors, and as fate would decide in years to come, they married after both Eges and Leo had passed away. She was 76, he was 52, when they eloped. He called her "Mama"; she called him "Papa". Neither had children. She was tall, slender, graying hair, but heavy boned, weighing about 200. He was slightly shorter with beautiful white hair, weighing about 160.

Sitting side by side, he would pat her knee or she would pat his. He worked while she stayed at home. During his breaks or dinner, he would call and check on "Mama". She did the laundry, cooking, fed chickens, and butchered. He took care of the acreage and held a job. He drove; she rode. She talked; he listened. She shot the gun through the roof to scare the intruder; he patched the roof and ceiling. She would laugh; he would smile. She told stories; he nodded.

The stigma of being on the Orphan Train and not knowing about his parents stayed with him. Many times, she patted his knee and said that she would have adopted him. They were perfectly matched, till death did they part.

From 1853 till 1929, homeless destitute waifs living on the streets of large cities, in poverty and woe, were placed on Orphan Trains. 250,000 children rode the iron rails that lullabied the homeless to sleep and disbursed them to unknown strangers. While not perfect, it served to provide homes, jobs, and/or room and board for the helpless. Most found families that loved them.

JULIE MARQUARDT

THE BEST SMITHY

Julie Marquardt is a haiku poet extraordinaire and a young adult author. Her current book project is about a sea-loving young lady from the 1800s who finds herself mixed up with pirates and other adventures. At the same time, she is awakening to the realization that she is quickly growing up and becoming a young lady, whether she wants to or not.

Formerly a nurse, Julie currently resides in Oklahoma, and writes whenever she can. She has a short story published in *Alternate Perspectives*. To learn more about Julie Marquardt and her projects, visit her webpage: www.wordsbyjulie.info.

.

THE BEST SMITHY

by Julie Marquardt

This is a love story, the story of Sam Whittaker and Bear Griffin. It is inspired by and dedicated to my parents, who fell in love as quickly as Sam and Bear did. They have been going strong for sixty-nine years - and counting.

Sam Whittaker was an oddity. First off, Sam's a girl, well a woman really, and a very large one at that. Her true name was Samantha, but that's quite a mouthful for folks to say, so she has been Sam, since day one. I was there at day one; I am Dr. William Tarrant, the town doctor, and I assisted her into this world twenty-two years ago.

Second off, Sam's a blacksmith. Now, I do not know if she was the only female blacksmith in the world, but she was the only one anyone around these parts had ever heard of. Sam's daddy, Ben Whittaker, was the blacksmith and liveryman for Beacon, but he passed on a few years back, and since Sam learned the business from him, she just naturally took over.

Folks looked a bit askance at that, at first, but

but we had all known Sam her whole life, so people accepted it pretty darn quick. Besides, she was the only game in the Indian Territory, so who else were we going to use?

The farmers and ranchers out here got no time for blacksmithing. Some of the bigger outfits had their own smithy, but they weren't for hire out, so Sam, it was. Folks were downright proud of her; Sam might be an oddity, but she was our oddity.

Sam was a fine-looking woman, and like I mentioned, a very large one. She stood six feet two inches tall in her socks, had big bones and muscles everywhere, which she needed, as a smithy. Her long black hair hung in a single braid down her back, and her blue eyes usually had a sparkle. She had a big smile and a big heart; you could hear her laugh clear across the street, and she would do anything for you. Much of the time, Sam wore trousers and a man's shirt, since skirts were not useful in a stable or around the forge.

The only family she had left was Granny Tobin, her late mama's mother, and they lived together in a small house behind the livery stable and blacksmith shop. Sam was the light of Granny's life, and she wanted nothing more in this world than for Sam to be happy.

And, Sam was happy. She had almost everything in life a woman could want. About the only thing Sam did not have, was a husband.

Most men were completely intimidated by Sam's size; she towered over them and outweighed many. She could whip the best at anything requiring muscle, she was just so strong. Sadly, for Sam, most men were not interested in a woman who could wrestle them to the ground.

It did not seem to bother Sam much, being alone. She said the right man was going to come along one day, and there was no use fretting about it. So she went on, running the livery, blacksmithing, and helping her Granny and anyone else that needed it.

Once a year, at the county fair, Sam entered the blacksmith competition. It ran for three days and encompassed everything a smithy does, from making four shoes and fitting them perfectly on a horse, to mending farm machinery and tools.

Sam loved everything about the competition and had been the champion the last two years running. It looked like she was right in line for the third year, too. So far, no one had entered that had been able to beat her in the past.

The morning of the first day of the competition there was a buzz among the participants and watchers that there was a late entry.

A man, a stranger, had come into town the previous night and arranged to join the competition. Seems he was a traveling blacksmith, going from town to town, visiting the farms and ranches between them to ply his trade. He stayed in an area a few days, or weeks even, however long it took to get all the work for the area done. Then he packed up his wagon and moved on to another area where his skills were needed. His name was Bear Griffin, and since it was his first time in this area, no one had ever heard of him before.

The whole town was gathered at the blacksmith shop, since that was where the competition was held. Folks quietly speculated about the stranger and waited excitedly for him to make an appearance. Would he be able to beat their champion, Sam Whittaker?

Suddenly a cowbell was heard, and from around the corner of the Red Dirt Saloon and Emporium, a huge ox lumbered, pulling a wagon. A giant of a man walked beside the wagon, a rope leading to the ox held lightly in his meaty hands. Attached to the wagon, the cowbell swayed, gently announcing their arrival.

The man was simply enormous, at least six feet five inches tall with broad shoulders and thick muscular arms and thighs. His chocolate brown hair was shaggy and covered his ears. A surprisingly neat goatee adorned his chin, topped by a trim mustache. The giant's big brown eyes were staring across the heads of the townsfolk, at the tall black haired, blue-eyed vision staring back at him. He was captured by the blueness of her eyes and the welcoming sparkle he saw in them. Her hands were on her hips, and she was grinning from ear to ear at him.

To herself, Sam was thinking, "Lordy, that is a fine figure of a man. He is the perfect size for me. I would never have to worry about squeezing him too hard; and handsome, to boot!"

Beside her, Granny whispered admiringly and somewhat breathlessly, truth be told, "Oh, Sam, look at that man!"

Sam whispered back, "I'm lookin', Granny, I'm lookin'!" She raised her voice, calling out, "I sure hope you are Bear Griffin."

"Yes, ma'am, I surely am," he said and started to ask, "And who might you be?"

A shout from the crowd made him tear his eyes away from the spectacular Amazon before him. He realized that while he was so busy staring at Sam, he almost walked himself, the ox and the wagon right into the crowd.

He pulled back on the rope, hollering, "Whoa, now, George", and the ox stopped placidly, blowing a big slobbery breath out onto those standing in front of him. "I'm sorry, folks, for not paying attention to where me and George was going."

He looked over again at the woman who had caught his attention, standing a head or two taller than everyone else. "I was distracted", he admitted, and knowing laughter acknowledged his statement. As he watched, she began striding toward him through the crowd.

When she reached him, she stuck out her hand, saying in a clear, firm voice. "My name is Sam Whittaker, and I am mighty glad to make your acquaintance, Mr. Griffin. Welcome to the blacksmith competition", she paused a moment, then added, "I am the current champion."

She was shaking his hand as she spoke, her big hand swallowed by his as she stared boldly into his amazing brown eyes.

Bear was thinking to himself, "Land sakes, this is one hell of a woman! Why, we're almost eye to eye. I cannot believe…wait, did she just say she is the current champion?"

"I'm pleased to meet you, ma'am, please call me Bear." He hesitated, finally blurting, "You are the current champion?"

"I am. Do you have a problem with that?" Sam inquired sweetly, not intimidated at all by the question.

"Why, no, ma'am, I just don't know that I ever heard of a lady blacksmith before. I surely hope you don't mind losing your title, 'cause that is what you're fixin' to do", he challenged her.

"Well, well, you are certainly sure of yourself, aren't you? We'll just have to see about that. I have no intention of giving up my crown. I hope you don't mind losing to a woman", she retorted. "And you can call me Sam." She suddenly realized she and Bear had been standing there holding hands the entire time. She smiled at him and gently took her hand back.

"Man or woman, makes no difference since I intend to win", he winked at her, then got down to business. "Where do you want me to put old George here?"

Sam showed him where to put the ox and wagon.

The contest began shortly thereafter, and for the next two days the competition was neck and neck between Sam and Bear as they steadily sent the other contestants to the sidelines. By the third and final day, it would be just the two of them, facing off.

When they were not competing, the pair spent every waking moment in each other's company, getting to know one another and very much liking what they learned. Neither had ever met anyone they were so compatible with. They liked the same things, and their dislikes were similar as well. Sam thought Bear lived up to his name, as he was big and lumbering in appearance, but could be gentle and cuddly, too.

As for Bear, he was sure Sam was the most beautiful creature, inside and out, on God's earth. He loved watching her, no matter what she was doing; he found her movements strong, yet graceful at the same time.

Best of all, and what they both loved, was the way Sam fit into Bear's embrace; physically, they fit together perfectly. Neither felt the other would be crushed just by hugging. In the past, both had to constantly rein in their strength, not wanting to bruise anyone in their enthusiasm. But Sam and Bear could, and did, wrap their arms tightly around each other and give true and heartfelt hugs. The first time she felt Bear's strong arms, squeezing her firmly, she sighed blissfully and hugged him right back.

"My, oh, my, I'm falling for you, Miss Sam Whittaker", he whispered into her hair. "I have loving feelings for you I never had for a woman before. I think you have the same feelings for me." He felt her nod and heard her murmured agreement, "Mmhm", against his neck. "So what are we going to do about it? Think you would be interested in marrying a fellow like me?"

He continued quickly, not giving her a chance to answer. "I know this is quick, and if you're not interested, I'll just mosey on, tomorrow, after the competition. But if you are interested, I'll stay here in Beacon—if you want me to—and we can go from there. You know, get to know each other more and make some plans. I'm ready to settle down…"

He knew he was babbling now, but could not seem to stop himself, so Sam lifted her head, placed both hands on either side of his face and gently, softly kissed his lips.

After savoring the kiss a moment, she leaned back, grinned and said, "You just plan on staying right here in Beacon, Mr. Bear Griffin. I love you, too, and I feel it deep and sure in my heart and soul. We are made for each other."

Bear let out a big huff of relief, "Hallelujah! Glad that's over! I was nervous as a cat to say anything so soon, but I surely am happy I did now." He pulled her forward for a longer kiss, and then they sat on the porch and talked for hours. They talked about what they wanted in a partner, what their plans were in life, where they would live, how they would live, and everything else they could think of. By the time Sam went into her little house, Granny had already gone to bed, so she had to wait until morning to share her exciting news.

Granny was, of course, thrilled beyond words, well, almost, when Sam told her she and Bear planned to marry.

"I knew it!" Granny crowed. "The whole town saw how you two looked at each other from the minute you met and haven't let the other out of your sight since then. I am so happy for you, honey." She hugged Sam hard.

"He's coming for breakfast, so we can all talk about it." Sam told her grandmother. "We want you to be a part of everything, too, Granny. You're all the family I have, and we're going to stick together, no matter what happens."

"Honey, I am not worried about me for a minute; I know you and Bear will take care of me, too. He's a fine man, Sam, and he'll do right by us. Does he have any family?" Before Sam could answer, there was a knock on the door and Granny said, "Well, I guess he can tell me himself", as Sam opened the door and let Bear in. Granny gave Bear a big hug, then told Bear and Sam to sit down at the table. She cooked and served up breakfast, then sat with them, and they talked as they ate together.

And so, Bear stayed in his wagon while they built onto the small house. They went straight up, building on a second story for Sam and Bear. Granny would stay in her room downstairs, warm and cozy, close to the kitchen where she was happiest.

Their wedding day came, and the whole town was there as they exchanged vows in front of the blacksmith shop. The barn doors stood open and were decorated with ribbons and greenery.

The crowd fanned out into the street, and I had the happy pleasure of walking Sam down the aisle formed by all the people who knew and loved her.

Everyone was pleased as punch our Sam had found such happiness, and they wholeheartedly welcomed Bear into their hearts and town.

After the ceremony, Bear moved into the house, and they became the first husband and wife blacksmith team ever heard of by anyone around here. About two years in, they started having children, and they're up to four or five by now; I lost count. I retired a couple of years ago, so it's not my job to keep count any more.

Oh, who won the blacksmith competition at the county fair that year, you ask? Well, funny, that. The last day was shoemaking day, and Sam and Bear hammered out every kind of horseshoe imaginable and shoed every horse in sight. Their holes were perfect in size and alignment, and every shoe fit perfectly.

In the end, the judges just could not pick one better than the other. So, Sam and Bear became the first Queen and King of the blacksmith competition, and that's another thing that had never been heard of by anyone around these parts!

CAROL NICHOLS

SARAH JACOBSON

Carol Nichols worked in the legal profession since her junior year of high school as a legal secretary for an El Reno law firm. She worked for the Canadian County Sheriff's Office under four different administrations and with the District Attorney's Office. After a move to Southern Illinois, she worked for a criminal defense attorney before moving to Pennsylvania. In Pennsylvania, Carol started writing through journals to deter loneliness caused by separation from family.

After returning to El Reno in 1992, she worked for USDA at Ft. Reno before retiring. Carol's journey continued with family illness and the death of her husband, Glen, thus heightening her awareness of life's fragility. Carol found release in writing and expresses her feelings about life, marriage and faith in her writings. She now resides in El Reno with her Jack Russell terrier, Patches.

SARAH JACOBSON
by Carol Nichols

Holding Momma close as I grasp Beth's hand, I walk from the graveyard as condolences were given to my family on the death of my father.

"Sarah, I'll see you at school, if possible." Miss Turner says while giving a pat on the back.

I straighten as I reply, "Yes, I will be there, as I will make it possible."

I didn't say "if possible"; no, I said with a non-defeated attitude "make it possible." "If" was my past way of life. Yes, IF never entered my mind, as life's hard times had not defeated me, not even dampened my spirits.

All that changed upon the death of my father. You see, I had been through all the grieving process, including many shed tears at my father's funeral where everyone said things like, "poor child" and "God have pity on you, sweetheart," which made me more determined than ever that tears would never be shown in public again.

I, Sarah Jacobson, was past tears, past mad and now was on to hate. Not hate for any person, but hate for circumstances that had been forced on me as the oldest sibling. Hate for being overlooked to the point of being kicked in the teeth for being born female instead of male.

Yes, I had often felt the sting of the words from my father as he would chuckle and say, "No, no sons for us, but God blessed us with Sarah." Really, I didn't feel like a blessing to anyone, and then, my father died. The loss to my mother was monumental as she sat on the side porch of the big two story house with a dazed look, often having to be reminded that she had children that still needed her care.

I didn't know what to do, as no words could penetrate the depth of sorrow in my mother's eyes. I would just love on my mother while slowly lifting her from her seated position. "Now, Momma," trying to be an encouragement, "you have to get up. Please, Momma, I have to leave for work."

Yes, thank you, Lord, for Judge Gresham. He was the family attorney before he became judge in our small community. He had taken pity on us, yes, pity as I saw it in his eyes. He wasn't the only person in our church congregation that felt that way, and I had often asked God to give me the opportunity and ability to change our circumstances.

As of that moment, I vowed I would never give anyone a reason to have pity on me or my family again. One Sunday at church, the Judge said, "Sarah, you graduate soon, don't you?"

"Well, yes, yes, Sir, I do."

"Please, drop by the office and visit with Bertha after school tomorrow, if your mother can spare you."

I was now thinking, *No, mother really couldn't spare me, and the only thing that has allowed me to stay in school is that Elizabeth was, by God's blessing, also in school.*

"Yes, Judge, I surely will." I smiled the big smile with which everyone had become accustomed.

"Good, I'll tell Bertha to expect you."

Judge Gresham definitely knew my family well. I certainly wouldn't be able to trust my mother, all alone, to the care of, not to mention, the safety of a smaller child. It wasn't all my mother's fault, though, as her life had handed her ample misery, and it seemed misery had won.

The large age difference in Elizabeth and me wasn't intentional. Baby after bay would be delivered stillborn after what seemed a normal pregnancy to the

the midwife, for Primghar had no doctor.

Each baby boy was now laid peacefully in Zion Church Cemetery. The long months of carrying the child, plus each pregnancy seemed to bring longer and harder labor to only have the child, long awaited, laid in my mother's arms, lifeless. Then, as my father stood at the end of her bed, he would give a name to his long awaited son. Momma would rock and sing to the child before the small lifeless body would be forcefully pulled from her. I had been shielded this scene for the first son, but as the frequency was repeated, neither of my parents seemed to notice that I was witnessing the events.

Upon Elizabeth's birth, Momma rejoiced at the lively baby, but Father turned with apparent disappointment, which did not go unnoticed by Mother. Her jubilance was short-lived and thus, it is my belief that that was when my once vibrant mother, who made me feel I was the joy of her life, began her withdrawal to her inside world, leaving me to care for our sweet Beth.

I didn't shrug from the job as I loved caring for her and the smell of her sweet innocence as I rocked her and quieted her fears. I now realize that I longed for this love and so needed it to replace my mother's love that was being stolen from me.

But now, I had to think about what I could wear to school that would be appropriate for a visit to the Judge's office.

I thought the school day would never end, and I thankfully was able to arrange for Beth to play with Billy Morgan as I left for the appointment at Judge Gresham's. Was I actually saying I would be entering an office of a Judge?

Stoically standing, I look at the brass handled glass double doors before me. I take a short step up onto a brass step, and the doors easily yield, revealing a marble entry which surprisingly is a short hall. On my immediate right is a millinery shop, which I might be able to walk into one day if the judge is going to offer me a job. Straight in front is a gunsmith, which was not at all provocative to a young adolescent.

As I look to my left, two doors with gold lettering in an arched manner announce the offices of Honorable George Gresham and Peter Honnicutt, Attorneys at Law. Entering the office, directly in front, I see a small desk but nonetheless a lavishly carved piece of furniture. A petite-framed woman is seated at her desk, wearing wire-rimmed glasses. In front of the desk are two matching dark rose-colored chairs.

"Excuse me, Miss Hunnish. I'm Sarah Jacobson, and Judge Gresham asked me to stop by after school so I may visit with you."

It is hard to keep my mind on my conversation with Miss Hunnish, as I have never been in, not to mention, could ever have dreamed of being in, such a palatial establishment. The tall ceilings are impeccably covered in a large number of smaller panels of highly polished fine wood. Each panel is bordered with numerous wood strips of differing heights, thus giving the appearance of smaller framed pictures. As the framed panel edges touch the outer walls, they are met by curved alcoves, which in turn lead to walls of huge panels that mimic the ceiling but on a far grander scale.

Returning my gaze to Miss Hunnish, who is obviously letting me absorb every richness. "Ma'am, I'm sorry. I didn't hear your last question."

"My dear, it wasn't a question. I merely asked you to be seated, for a moment, while I attend to completing my document."

"Yes. Ma'am, thank you." I really want to say, *Oh thank you, thank you for giving me further opportunity to continue absorbing this opulence.*

While seated, I can look at the many portraits of people, of which I have no idea who they possibly could be, but I definitely know they are people of prominence due to their attire and the extravagant wood-carved chairs in which some are seated. I shift in my seat to get a further view of the room and also simultaneously glance to Miss Hunnish and see I am of no concern to her as she toils over her document.

To my far left are glass-faced wooden cabinets containing, what seems to me, an enormous amount of leather-bound books. To my right are three sets of doors, which are paneled identical to the walls but having gold lettering identifying each office.

"Sorry, Miss Jacobson, but these documents need to be filed at the courthouse today. Please come and walk with me so we may visit."

I arise without a word and hold one of the large doors for Miss Hunnish to exit.

"Thank you very much, Sarah. That was very sweet of you."

Now falling behind, I am quickly admonished by Miss Hunnish as she says, "Child, get up here, and don't dawdle."

I rush forward, as my arm is abruptly grabbed, halting my advance, just as a horse and carriage rushes by on the cobblestone street. "Sarah, if I hadn't stopped you, you would have most certainly been trampled!"

I flip my one golden braid to the back, straighten my skirts, and we continue across to the courthouse square. As we begin the climb up the first set of steps in the courtyard, I look up at the three-story O'Brien County Courthouse sitting aloof and regal, in the center of Primghar. Inside, the marble floors immediately disappear to my right and left as Miss Hunnish, with gusto, continues straight forward without a glance in either direction to the first open bar area where she says, "Agnus, how are you, this fine afternoon?"

Agnus, answering but never making eye contact with Miss Hunnish as her gaze is on me, says, "Who might this be?"

"Oh, this is—child, tell the lady your name!"

"I'm Sarah Jacobson. Pleased to make your acquaintance," as I add a small curtsy, in the hope of staying in the good graces of both women.

Continuing to the next open window, Miss Hunnish says, "Hello, Sally, how are you?"

"I'm doing well, and you?" Without letting Miss Hunnish reply, she swiftly continues, "Bertha, it seems there was an altercation last evening between the Wilson boy and the Jacobs boy. Have you heard anything? Was Mr. Honnicutt summoned to the Sheriff's Office?"

Miss Hunnish, looking down her nose at Sally, says, "Why, Sally Harper, you know I would never divulge any such information," shrugging toward me, while whipping her skirts to the rear as she turned and advanced across the marble floors and the next area.

Thinking to myself, I wonder if the conversation with Miss Harper would have had the same outcome if I were not present.

Our short trip across the hall is obviously our correct destination, as the documents are signed into a large book and filed with the clerk.

Now exiting the building, I dutifully follow Miss Hunnish down the steps, but I an now being cautious as I hear hooves approaching on the cobblestone street.

Miss Hunnish walks purposefully to the general store where the gentle jingle of the bells announce our entrance, and I am met by the gaze of a blue-eyed, sandy-haired boy, kneeling and placing items on a shelf. I immediately flush and turn away, only to be prodded once more by Miss Hunnish.

"Good afternoon, Mr. Palmer," Miss Hunnish begins, but that is all that I comprehend as I look intently at the blonde-haired boy, wondering why I have not seen him in school or church.

My wayward daydream is brought to a sharp halt as I hear Miss Hunnish say, "Oh, add a couple of more items, Mr. Palmer. Three pencils and a gummy eraser. No, make that two gummy erasers as Miss Jacobson will certainly need two erasers, won't you, Miss Jacobson?"

Had I heard Miss Hunnish correctly? Could this possibly mean I am to be employed in the Judge's office?

"Oh, where are my manners? Mr. Palmer, this is Miss Sarah Jacobson. Miss Jacobson is soon to graduate from Primghar High school and will be assisting at the law office. It seems that Miss Jacobson has touched a soft spot in Judge Gresham's heart."

I again feel my face flush as I lower my eyes, knowing I am being watched.

"Well, Miss Jacobson, it will be a pleasure to assist you anytime there is a need," states Mr. Palmer with confidence that the opportunity would certainly occur.

Miss Hunnish continues, "There will be a need, in the near future, for William to move some boxes of books, if you would be so kind in letting him assist. One of Miss Jacobson's immediate duties is making room in the Law Library for the new law books and journals as they arrive."

"I see no problem in that as long as it isn't the first of the month or a Friday," adds Mr. Palmer. Looking in William's direction, he continues, "William, please come over, so you may be introduced to Miss Jacobson."

William, standing from his crouched position, maneuvers the glass front cases toward me and Miss Hunnish, as I recognize the boy's full height and think, "Finally, a boy taller than myself."

Mr. Palmer, with a wide grin, says, "William Franklin, this is Miss Jacobson." As Mr. Palmer states, "I'm sorry, I don't know your first name?"

Miss Hunnish jumps in the conversation saying, "Allow me! Sarah Jacobson, this is Mr. Franklin."

William gives a slight bow toward me. I give a slight curtsy toward William as we each feel our faces turning dark red—from what? Excitement?

Miss Hunnish hands me the wrapped items that have been purchased, as we bid good day and exit the store.

The final week of school flies as graduation approaches, and preparation for the outdoor ceremony looms on the horizon. The Summit Township School District Class of 1880 is a small one with four girls and five boys. A new dress is out of the question for me, but I would not let that hamper the jubilance I feel for my new job, a job that will bring money into our house and possibly repay some of the people that have stood by the Jacobson Family. I shiver as I think of the number of receipt books that are stacked in a cubby at the grocery with my family's name on the end of each.

I have sold the buggy and tried to keep Old Lucy, but she had to be sold eventually, also. The milk cow, chickens and rabbits have been the our mainstays.

And, thank you, Lord, I can wring the chickens' neck and hang them on the clothesline beside the rabbit I am skinning, without flinching in the process.

Maybe this winter, I can afford to have wood instead of scavenging for cow patties to burn.

Other children my age would be running and playing, but not me. No, the hand that I, Sarah Jacobson, had been dealt will be played, for I am certain God has something in store for me beyond my wildest imagination. Whenever I start to feel the slightest tinge of fear, I remember my father's words. "No, no boys for us, but we have Sarah." How could those words that stung so deeply be the same words that seem like a rebel call to arms? Yes, I'm not that child any longer; I am a woman, a woman that has been so incensed by life that the tomorrows of tomorrow can hold no fear.

"Sarah, where are you going?"

"Momma, you remember, don't you, at church yesterday when Judge Gresham patted you on the back and told you how he really appreciated you being able to spare me so I could work at his office? You remember? Beth will be here with you, and I'll be back later in the day." While I embrace her, I softly whisper, "You know I love you, Momma, and I'll always take care of you and Beth."

Oh Lord, why do I feel guilty every time I leave the house? Is it because of the heaviness that is lifted from my soul upon starting down the street toward Jensen's corner? Yes, I don't have to go this way to town, but when I turn down the lane, I know I am going to pass the willow by the creek bank standing so majestically and then the pear tree so laden, and I am able to get a pear for my lunch. I find myself praying a thank you prayer to you, Lord, every day for your blessing. This small moment of escape from the reality of life is enough to bolster me, or is it what bolsters my self-worth, for, Lord, if you care for these stately trees, how much more is your love for me?

Pulling my skirts up, I ran forward with a lighthearted feeling as I look ahead to another day with a purpose, a day that includes me and William Franklin alone in the Judge's Law Library!

SHANE SMITH

A FEATHER IN THE RAIN

Shane Smith is the author of *The First and The Last*, a heroic fantasy and parable. He is currently working on a prequel as well a horror novel, *The Laboratory of Doctor Lazuro*. A gifted philosophical poet and short story writer, Shane resides in El Reno, OK with his wife, his daughter, and his pet dragon named Rudy.

A FEATHER IN THE RAIN

by Shane Smith

She loved the sky, especially at night - hues of blue, violet, and orange moving slowly over her head. Her people saw the sky different than the rest of the world. All was holy, all was sacred, and all were siblings by heart. She even considered a bear to be her brother, though she never got too close.

Her name was Rainfeather, and she was a native to this land. This meant two things, one of which was her love for life. Every single day was an adventure: rocky hills to climb, porcupines to chase, rivers to swim—everything was just perfect.

The other thing it meant was that her heart overflowed with nothing but kindness, as did the hearts of the rest of her village. They claimed ownership over nothing and no one. All were free, and all were one, especially when it came to the land. But that was all about to change.

Rumor had spread amongst the various tribes that some members of the white tribe—that nobody in the village had met before—were leaving their homesteads and lingering near the natives.

It was said by the chief and the medicine men that this was an omen of something powerful, though whether for ill or for good, they did not know. Some believed that the whole of the white tribe were generous and trustworthy, but the majority thought they were ruthless and destructive. Certain groups of them had been driving the Indians from their homes for hundreds of years, and there were tales of isolated incidents involving the pillaging and complete decimation of villages.

But Rainfeather bore no ill will. She knew that not all of the white men were murderous. She also knew that a good number of people from the major Native tribes had actually been the ones to instigate the fighting. In her mind, as well as in the minds of her mother and father, there was no difference between the Indian and the white man.

Things like color, creed, and clan didn't really matter. All were brothers, and all had a potential for good as well as for evil. But though she had met white men before, these new ones were strangers, and she had enough sense to at least be cautious.

Her village itself was isolated from all the others. They had no quarrel with any other villages, and they even had festivals with villages from totally different tribes on occasion, but they mostly kept to themselves.

Now, however, they were going to have to confront the white men, for the newcomers would wander into the settlement and stare silently, which frightened the children. The chief, who was Rainfeather's uncle on her father's side, approached the men, with three warriors at each of his sides. Yes, these warriors were skilled in the art of combat, but, unlike the Pequot and the Comanche, they had never before been involved with fighting the white colonists. Still, if worst came to worst, the chief was confident that they could defend the village well, even though the worst this particular village ever had to deal with in the past was a strong persistence by the colonists to convert the natives to a different God.

Rainfeather, crouched behind the rocks she had been climbing all day, watched the meeting silently, her heart pounding with anticipation. She was a good distance away from the village, but she could still witness the events very clearly.

Her uncle began speaking to the three white men,

who had been standing atop a grassy hill for half an hour. Despite having an accent, his English skills were excellent, something he shared to an extent with Rainfeather. She wasn't quite as fluent as he was, but she could still understand most of what was now being said.

"Welcome," began the chief. "May we extend our hands to you, gentlemen? Do you need food or shelter?"

The white men stood with stoic faces and remained silent for at least a minute. After that, the chief began speaking again.

"Do you—"

"Yes," said the man in the middle, their apparent leader, as he began to stroke the brim of his wide hat. He was significantly larger than the others. "We need food and shelter." His two companions started to snigger, and the sniggering morphed into loud hooting and hollering within seconds. The man in the middle just smiled.

Though he was filled to the brim with suspicion and anxiety, the chief resumed with his kind words.

"All that we have is yours. The women are—"

"You're goddamn right about that," snarled the man to the left of his leader. The one on the right began laughing hysterically, then reached for something clipped to his belt.

The six Indian warriors each gripped the long knives at their belts and jolted forward slightly, but the chief held them back by raising his hand.

The white man on the right stared straight into the eyes of the warriors. "Typical," he whispered. He then lifted the object from his belt, a flask, to his face and poured the contents down his throat. The Natives recoiled ever so slightly from the smell of the whiskey.

"Do you—" said the chief, before being cut off once again.

"Speaking of the women," drawled the leader of the cowboys. "All you have is ours. Ain't he generous, boys?"

Their hysterical hollering was quickly drowned out by the warning cries of several sentry warriors along the perimeter of the village. They were engaged in battle with a score of cattlemen who had appeared out of nowhere from all sides. The sentries had been prepared from the beginning - but in this case, it didn't matter.

At these cries of warning, the chief and two of his warriors turned their heads towards the settlement to see what was happening. The three of them were shot down by pistols immediately, dying instantly. Rainfeather gasped as tears began to run down her face.

As the three brave Native Americans were shot, the remaining four of the warriors sprung forward and felled two of the white men with their knives in one swift motion. They had aimed for the leader, but the man had leapt backwards with lightning speed. He drew his pistol and shot the four of them, less than a second after they had killed his two comrades.

Rainfeather was paralyzed by a mix of despair, anger, fear, and guilt. She thought, however irrationally, that if only she had been there with her uncle, six members of her community wouldn't have lost their lives. She knew how to fight, thanks to the guidance of her brother throughout her youth, and she immediately began to despise herself for not pointing her arrows at the men while remaining unseen.

She had her bow strung now, though, not letting the shock of the situation dominate her for more than a few seconds. As she looked down from her vantage point, it seemed that the whole village was screaming. Not all of the screams came from her kinsfolk, but most of them did.

The sounds of the village crying out in pain from gun blasts permeated the air and gave it a sickly thickness.

A death cry from the cowboys would be heard every now and then, but it would always be eclipsed by the anguished cries of the Indian victims.

This village wasn't like other tribes. They didn't have guns for themselves - only bows and knives. Regret filled the hearts of them all, even though their hearts were righteous. Regret for staying isolated. Regret for staying kind. Regret for being peaceful.

The village sentries fought valiantly but were quickly swept up in a cyclone of gunpowder. Yes, the villagers outnumbered the white men - but what good was that against an onslaught of shotguns and six shooters?

Rainfeather pulled back the string of her bow - only to feel a sharp thud at the back of her head and fall unconscious. She awoke a few hours later to find herself within the tent of her uncle.

While this would normally be a joyous and highly spiritual occasion, it was far from it, this time.

Six cowboys stood over her, while members of her family lay bound and tethered beside her. They were all women and elders. Rainfeather's stomach sank at the thought of the young warriors of the village. She knew that they were probably all dead by now.

"Look at these animals," said one of the cowboys. "They're ready to be tamed."

It was then that Rainfeather noticed her mother, tied up a mere two meters away. The woman looked at her daughter, but at the same time, she wasn't looking at her. Bruises and blood covered her face as her eyes grew darker and darker with resignation. All hope had been beaten out of her.

"Mother!" cried Rainfeather. "Mother!"

One of the cowboys seemed to grow excited by this desperate moment. He picked up the old woman and began to hit her without mercy. Rainfeather, however, along with four other women in the tent, wasn't tied up at all. The men didn't think it necessary, for the girls were all under sixteen years of age.

They were about to find a huge flaw in their drunken logic. In a flash, Rainfeather leapt from the floor and threw herself at the despicable attacker. The momentum of the jump pinned him down just long enough for Rainfeather to grab the pistol at his belt and shoot him in the neck. Though she had never before used a gun, the act was still remarkably easy.

Before the other five men could react, she shot up

like a rattler and fired at two of them, killing them instantly. The remaining three were shooting at her simultaneously, but the first dead man's body made for her an excellent shield. She dropped the gun and ran with the body out of the tent with more strength than she had ever possessed in her life, threw the man down, and disappeared behind the trees.

As she ran further into the woods, her heart filled with regret over not taking her mother with her, but the rational part of her knew that it would have been impossible. No, Rainfeather needed to hide and bide her time, waiting for the right moment to strike and free her community.

The sounds of the men pursuing her were growing louder as they began to catch up. In a last ditch effort, she clambered up a tree with the agility of a squirrel, and there she waited, praying that the men wouldn't find her. Her prayers seemed to have been answered as she watched the men approach her tree, linger for a few seconds, and then split up to cover more ground. The fact that they didn't see her in the branches above was nothing short of a miracle.

She closed her eyes, breathed heavily, and thanked the Creator, but her respite was short-lived. Within a minute, two of the men came back and stood at the base of the tree. Even though she was twenty feet above them, she could still hear every word spoken.

"Where the hell is she?" asked the taller of the two.

"I don't know, Will," answered the other. "Damn savages are crafty."

They were looking up at the branches of the trees. As their piercing eyes scanned closer to her hiding place, Rainfeather silently pulled a small dagger from her moccasin. She threw it with all her might at the one called Will. He cried out briefly as the blade severed his jugular, then fell to the earth at his companion's feet.

The surviving man was given no time to react as Rainfeather pounced on him from high above. She thrust his own gun into his neck, right as he began to pull the trigger.

Though the men were now dead, Rainfeather was far from safe. The commotion had attracted several more cowboys, who were running hard towards their fallen comrades. When they got there, however, the brave woman was nowhere to be seen, having already climbed into the branches of an even taller tree nearby.

"Jenkins and Will are dead! How the hell did she do it?"

"Looks like she got Will with a knife. Jenkins was shot."

"Where the hell did she get a gun? The girl's just a child! How could she—"

"Wait, John."

"I'm just saying, how in God's name could she—"

"Shut up. Jenkins' gun ain't on him."

The men stood still and silent for a few seconds. It was during this pause that Rainfeather noticed a sharp pain in her left calf and the moisture from a warm fluid running down her leg.

She had been shot during her initial escape, and her sheer adrenaline had kept her from noticing it. Both her adrenaline and her heartbeat were still very high, but they were now accompanied by pain and lightheadedness. She knew she wouldn't last long with the amount of blood she was losing, so she had to do something fast to save her village.

As she began planning her attack, heavy rustling could be heard within the brush nearby, along with the sound of heavy, metallic footfalls.

They were coming from a large man wearing heavy steel-toed boots. As he drew nearer, Rainfeather realized that he was none other than the leader whom her uncle had approached atop the hill. All the sounds of the forest seemed to cease abruptly at his sheer presence. Even his own men seemed to slightly lower their shoulders in submission to their hulking, bearded leader.

"We're gonna find her, boys," he said darkly, "and then, I'm gonna teach her a real good lesson in respect."

Two of the men began to chuckle quietly, but the third responded to his leader with disagreement.

"I don't know, boss. She killed our men. We gotta take her out real slow like...make her feel it, ya know?"

"No, Boothby. This little lady is a jewel. She's got more spunk than a lotta men I've known."

"But—"

"A prize. One worth earning."

The prize herself was sick of this. She couldn't bear their voices any longer, and she knew she was on the brink of death. In her mind, it was time to go out fighting...so she began. Bullets rained down from high above their heads, and two of them were hit in the chest. Rainfeather had good aim, but she still missed the other two, who were remarkably fleet of foot. They immediately fired their own shots in her direction, loudly splintering her shelter of wood. Rainfeather began to realize how old and frail this tree truly was as her branch snapped from the trunk. She held on for dear life as both she and the limb crashed down below onto the dead men's bodies.

After a brief daze, she looked up to see the lead cowboy looking down on her. She aimed the gun between his eyes and pulled the trigger.

Nothing. She frantically tried to shoot, over and over again, as the man began to laugh a deep and sinister laugh.

"All outta bullets, darlin'? That's all right. No use fightin' no more. Come here."

He reached down to grab her by the hair but stopped as the forest erupted with the sound of gunfire and hoofbeats. The man turned around to have his skull smashed in by the swift front legs of a horse. Atop the animal's back was another cowboy. He was clean-shaven and didn't appear to be as dirty as the other cattlemen, but Rainfeather still feared him as he peered down into her eyes.

Six other horses trotted into view, and several other new men were running on foot in between them.

"Jim," one of them shouted, "we got 'em all. Every last sorry one of 'em."

The man above Rainfeather leapt off of his horse and looked at the other man briefly.

"And the Injuns?"

"We untied 'em, Jim. But they're all afraid of us. Damn outlaws made sure of that."

Jim looked back at Rainfeather and began to approach her.

"It's okay, sweetheart," he began. "No one's gonna hurt ya now. You're safe."

Rainfeather was nearly unconscious, but she still mustered up enough strength to back far away from the man. He stopped approaching her then and stood there with sadness in his eyes.

"Don't even try," said another man. "She cain't understand ya anyways."

"Understand," moaned Rainfeather painfully. "I do understand."

Jim smiled with relief.

"That's swell," he said. "That's just swell, little lady. We ain't gonna let them hurt ya no more. They were outlaws—criminals. Real bad men, ya hear?"

Rainfeather held onto her consciousness with all her strength.

"They," she began, "they look the same as you. You're also devils."

Jim bent down and stroked her cheek.

"No, sweetheart. We're gonna getcha back on yer feet, then leave ya alone. Okay?"

"Mother!" she cried. "Where is my mother? Where is my father?"

And with that, consciousness fled from the woman who would soon come to be known as "The Girl with Bear Strength."

SUE D. L. SMITH

THE COWBOY FROM HELL

Sue D. L. Smith is a gifted writer and editor with a strong philosophical flair and varied life experiences that show in her short stories and fiction. A Master Gardener and a photographer (see cover photo), she is a true Renaissance woman. Sue recently returned to college and currently lives with her spouse and two cats in El Reno, OK.

THE COWBOY FROM HELL

by Sue D. L. Smith

Buford was a young man raised in the backwoods of Tennessee. He'd been whipped with belts as far back as he could remember, and it had made him mean and angry. His pappy would lay into him every time he came home from his job at the regional sawmill. Buford's pappy took his frustrations out on Buford every chance he got. If Buford didn't have the right tone in his voice or the right look in his eyes, his pappy (Willie was his name) would take him out to the shed and give him a lickin'.

Buford grew up so full of rage and hate that his mother and sisters were afraid of him. His teacher was afraid of him. But his pappy was not afraid of him. Buford tried to scare his pappy a time or two, but his pappy would lay into him and beat him to a whimpering pulp when he tried. Buford didn't think he could take living at home anymore. He was ashamed of himself and his weakness. Why couldn't he fight back? Why did his pappy always get the best of him?

One day at school, the teacher read a story in the

one-room schoolhouse about cowboys in Texas and how they herded cattle on long cattle trails and roped and branded steers and calves and heifers. Buford thought that just might be the life he was looking for.

Getting out in the fresh air away from the shack he and his family lived in sounded real good to him, being outside of any building sounded real good to him, and getting as far away from his pappy as he could sounded especially good to him. Buford's family had never herded or raised any cattle, but he figured he'd like them. They had to be nicer than any human, any day.

Every student through every grade through high school attended the one-room schoolhouse where Buford went. They all sat in the same classroom. The teacher, Miss Sally, taught all the subjects for all the grades and taught them well. She was a worn-out, spinster-looking woman who would arrive at the schoolhouse well before the students showed up, would stoke the fire and get it going, would sweep and mop the hardwood floor, and would clean the chalkboard.

Miss Sally also prepared something to eat for herself and anyone else in need in the mornings and at lunchtime.

She would have a kettle of food ready when the children arrived at school, and she kept one for lunchtime too, because many times the kids' bellies would growl loud enough to be heard, and many times they had not eaten a breakfast or brought a lunch for noontime. Miss Sally had a hard job, but she enjoyed instilling some education into these hill people of Tennessee.

Buford graduated from his country school at just barely eighteen. Buford decided after his class's small graduation ceremony that he would be leaving Tennessee right away. His mother would probably cry, but he had to go. His sisters would be glad to have one less mouth in the house to feed, he felt sure. Buford had gotten pretty big for his age, and it took a lot to feed his lanky frame now. Buford knew he was a burden to his family, and he wanted to get away and move on. His dad wouldn't miss him, he was sure, but he might miss having someone to beat on with his belt all the time. Buford wondered who his target would be after he left. He hoped it wouldn't be his mother.

Buford's mother Mary was a petite woman. She had been pretty in her day, but seven children and a brutish husband had taken any spark of beauty out of her face long ago. She endured her husband Willie because her mammy had told her, "You made your bed; you lie in it."

Willie (short for William) had been in the Civil War as a Confederate soldier, and he was mean as hell. But he had sweet-talked Mary, a 16-year-old with stars in her eyes, into letting him court her many years before while he was still in the confederacy. It wasn't long after they wed, however, that his true colors began to show.

Mary didn't know what to think about this husband of hers. She eventually resigned herself to her fate. She cringed whenever Willie would beat on Buford, but she remembered the saying in the *Bible* "spare the rod, spoil the child." She didn't dig any deeper than that. She figured Willie knew what he was doing as the man of the home. All she could do was be passive. But sometimes a fire would burn in her, and she would want to strike Willie with the iron poker she used to stir the ashes in the fireplace. She had done that once, and Willie had sent her flying across the room.

After that, she was a cowed woman. Willie needed someone to pummel, and that was just the way it was.

Buford grew up full of rage and hate. He hated his father—"Pappy"—as he called him. But Buford knew that hatred was not good.

In school, the teacher would read *Bible* verses to the children in the morning before she would begin the lessons for the day. Buford learned from her that hatred was akin to murder. How could he stop this fire burning in his heart that he held towards his pappy? His only solution seemed to be to leave home, and his mind was made up.

Buford left home the next day after graduating. His mother gave him a peck on the cheek and handed him a pole with a large napkin of food tied to it that he could carry over his shoulder as he headed off to his new life. Buford didn't have much feeling for his mom or his sisters anymore, but surprisingly he knew he would miss them.

His sisters all waved good-bye at the door, and a few of them cried. There were a lot of mouths to feed still, and Buford knew his leaving would only lessen the burden a little.

Willie scowled at Buford from the doorway as Buford told his mother and sisters good-bye as they stood outside in the bare front yard.

A few chickens were scratching in the dirt nearby. Willie gruffly yelled to Buford to mind he stayed out of trouble and not to give anybody any lip.

He then hollered "Good-bye!" after which he yelled to Buford, "and don't hurry back!"

Buford glared at him and hollered, "I'll be sure to stay away forever, if I can!" His pappy guffawed at what Buford said, laughing as he slapped his thigh, then turned around and went back inside the shack.

Buford couldn't understand why his pappy couldn't show any kind of love. Even animals had more love for their offspring than that man he called his "pappy." Buford figured his pappy must have something missing in his head, that he must be a little "tetched," as the saying went.

Buford suddenly surprised himself by giving his mother a quick hug, then turned on his heel and left. He looked back once to see his mother burying her face in her apron, her shoulders shaking with sobs. At least SHE would miss him. That—or she would miss him as the family scapegoat.

That made Buford mad just thinking about it. Yeah, he was just the whipping-post for the whole family's sins. Buford stomped all the way down the hill from his family's shack. *I'll get even one day,* he thought. *Yeah, they'll all be sorry they hurt me.*

At the bottom of the hill, Buford turned left. He was headed for Texas, but he needed to stop in town and see if anyone was going in that direction who might let him tag along. He would work for his food and keep and owe no one a thing. He would be free as a bird and see the countryside and not have to think about what he was leaving behind.

The sun was rising in the sky as Buford headed to the general store. There he saw the general store owner, Mr. Lanyard, sweeping the front stoop. He waved at him and sped up his walk. Mr. Lanyard leaned on his broom and watched Buford approach. He knew this boy and a little bit about his situation, and he felt sorry for him. Buford's father was a mean 'un, and Mr. Lanyard never wanted to make him mad, because Willie could make life hell for a person.

Mr. Lanyard waved to Buford and waited. Buford was a little out of breath in his haste, and Mr. Lanyard invited him to come in and set a spell near the stove and have something hot to drink. Buford's eyes lit up. That sounded real good to him.

The morning was cool and autumn was settling in, and a hot cup of something would sure warm his insides.

All he had on his back was what he was taking on his journey, and it was just a light jacket over an old plaid shirt and bib overalls, or "slops".

Buford followed Mr. Lanyard inside the store and sat down on a wooden bench near the hot stove. Mr. Lanyard handed him a cup of fresh-brewed coffee that his wife Sarah had made. Buford thanked Mr. Lanyard and took the hot cup of brew gingerly in his hands. Mr. Lanyard joined him on a seat nearby, and Buford told him what he was aiming to do. Mr. Lanyard told Buford that folks were always passing through town on their treks west, and if Buford wanted to spend a few days there at the general store and help him around the place, he was welcome to stick around. Surely someone would be passing through any day now on their way to Texas and take him along on their journey.

Buford thanked Mr. Lanyard for his kindness and told him he would do whatever they needed around the store. Mr. Lanyard told him he had a bed out back in the store and that he could sleep there. His missus would feed him, too. He could work for room and board and might even earn a little money to take on his trip. Buford was grateful for Mr. Lanyard's kindness and told him so.

Mr. Lanyard patted him on the shoulder and said he would be glad to have him around as long as he felt like staying. Buford flinched when Mr. Lanyard patted him on the shoulder. He wasn't used to any male touching him in a nice way. But then he relaxed. Mr. Lanyard seemed like a really nice man. Buford's heart was starting to thaw just a little bit toward humanity.

That evening, Mrs. Lanyard served up supper, which consisted of corn pone, grits, a hunk of ham, some collard greens, and biscuits and gravy. Buford hadn't eaten this good ever in his life. When he cleaned his plate, Mrs. Lanyard gave him second helpings. Buford's stomach hadn't ever been this full before. His still-growing body latched onto every morsel that entered his mouth.

Finally, after cleaning his second plate of food, Buford gave a sigh of satisfaction and leaned back in his chair, pushing his cleaned plate to the side. This was the first time he had ever had enough food to eat, and he couldn't eat one more bite.

Mrs. Lanyard looked happily at her husband. They had never had children of their own, and it gave them both some satisfaction watching this hungry young man eat. Mrs. Lanyard usually had dinner alone with her husband.

This was new to both of them, and they gave each other secret smiles of pleasure.

There was something likeable about this boy Buford. Mrs. Lanyard's heart was melting, and her voice was soft when she spoke to Buford. She asked Buford what it was like at home, and Buford told her, "It was all right." Then he looked off to the side and out a window. He didn't want to answer any more of her questions. Mrs. Lanyard knew in her heart that Buford had not had the best upbringing. Her husband had mentioned Willie a time or two, and she knew he was bad news. But Willie had never abandoned his family, and that said something for him. A lot of men would have left long ago if they'd had seven kids to rear in this difficult mountain terrain.

Mrs. Lanyard leaned forward at the table and asked Buford what he was aiming to do. Buford told her he wanted to go to Texas and be a cowboy. Mrs. Lanyard told Buford she thought that sounded real nice. Buford's eyes had lit up when he talked about the open range and being outdoors and away from people. Buford told her he didn't think he would mind being around cattle.

His face softened when he talked about the starry skies and moonlit nights he would see in Texas while lying on a blanket staring up in wonderment at all of God's glorious creation.

Mrs. Lanyard got up from the table and cleared the dishes. Buford jumped up and walked with her to the sink and helped her dry dishes while she washed. He told her he rightly enjoyed the meal she cooked. Mrs. Lanyard smiled with pleasure and told him "Thank you." It was nice to get a compliment from someone besides her husband, albeit her husband always complimented her cooking. She took pride in feeding the two of them and did her best, and she was glad to feed the extra mouth of this growing young man, too.

That night in bed, Buford lay with his arms folded back under his head. He was thinking really hard.

He really liked it here at the Lanyards' place. He wondered if maybe, just maybe, they might take him on as hired help. Texas was starting to sound far, far away. Maybe it was too far away. Things were right nice here in this small town, living away from under his pappy's roof. Perhaps being a cowboy wasn't what he was cut out to be. Maybe he'd stay…that is, if they'd let him.

Buford slowly drifted off to sleep with a smile on his face. He was leaving hell behind.

HART TILLETT

RUSHING CLOUD

Hart Tillett was born in British Honduras (Belize). He graduated from Carleton University (Canada) with an honors degree in Economics and thereafter devoted his professional life to banking and insurance. He plays cricket, enjoys horseback riding, is a chess enthusiast and open water scuba diver. His entry "Yoli" placed third in the NOSTALGIA category of the 2015 writing contest sponsored by the Oklahoma City Writers, Inc. Hart lives in Belize but resides for much of the year in Oklahoma City. He and his wife have four children.

RUSHING CLOUD

by Hart Tillett

Thwack! Fetellson, who had been dozing lightly following his evening meal, was instantly awake, alert and listening. Out here on the Nebraska prairie, sounds were a man's closest allies, and that of an arrowhead imbedding in the cabin wall was one that got his attention, as well as Mutt, his Bluetick coonhound. He counted the seconds, and on ten, he heard the whoosh of the second arrow followed by another thwack as the stone arrowhead embedded itself in the soft cedar shingle near his bedroom window.

Before the quivering arrow could stabilize, he was out of bed preparing to go meet his Paiute friend Rushing Cloud. As an unannounced Indian was likely to be shot on sight by a rider who did not know him, the signals were a way for him to alert Fettelson of his presence from a safe distance. The two-arrow signal meant that trouble was brewing for his or any of the one hundred and fifty-odd "swing-stations" that dotted the Pony Express route.

Rushing Cloud would be waiting for him under the aspen overhanging Blue Creek.

Hayland Fetellson was forty-seven years old, a Kentuckian by birth, who had become a drifter ever since his wife left him whilst he was serving a five-year jail sentence in Kansas. After his release, he had done range work in Wyoming, before joining the growing hordes that sought their fortunes in the gold-laden mountains of California.

That didn't work out, and when the new Pony Express people put out "Want Ads" for riders and station tenders, he applied and got a job as a swing station tender.

"Why would a man your age want to be out there alone?" the young agent had asked him when he presented himself to the company's office in San Francisco. Hayland studied him for a moment.

"Because you won't find anyone better than me for the job," he had replied. He let his eyes sweep the empty waiting room. "Or anyone else," he added with a twinkle of hazel eyes that gazed fixedly into those of the younger man. A week later he was on the stagecoach to the "Sand Hill" station.

His nearest contact with the rest of the world was thirty miles to the east in Guevarra, and Sagebrush twenty-two miles west. He was most suited for the job, having no family, tremendous survival skills which included a working knowledge of the Plains languages and knowing how to take care of himself.

His duties were simple. As stock tender, he was to feed and curry the horses and have fresh ones saddled and waiting for the incoming riders during the day. Riders, there were always riders, young boys mostly risking their lives for the American dream. As one rider raced in from the east, blowing lustily at the horn that they each carried, another would come in throwing up billows of dust from the west, each with his mochila containing the letters. They only had time to change horses. It was a matter of pride amongst the boys to try and beat the nine-hour target for the ride to California.

It was on one of his two monthly rest days that he had gone to Blue Creek to swim and do his laundry. A young man lay in the stream with a broken foot—an Indian. His horse stood by, nickering softly.

From the face markings, he knew the boy was Moapat from the Muddy Creek Paiute tribe, and the short parallel marks on his forehead told him that he was someone related to the Paiute warrior Chief Hagatatte. Mutt would have rushed the youth, but Hayland signaled him to be quiet.

"Never trust the Injuns," he had been warned, and he knew that there was good reason the Reds hated the white man. But this was different. The youth was in pain and would most likely die from drowning or exhaustion, if he didn't do something to help him. But what could he do? Company regulations forbade him to give accommodation to an Indian, and even if he wanted to, the cabin was too small to keep him there for any length of time without the riders knowing.

In any event, he had taken the youth back to his cabin, set the fracture amidst howls that could be heard as far as the next swing station, and bandaged it.

"What's your name?" he had asked the limping man in Paiute, as he helped him onto the bare back of his pony.

"Rushing Cloud," he had responded. "Everyone calls me Cloud."

"From these parts?" he urged, when the boy had said no more. There was a slight hesitation as the lad thought about the question. "I just need to know how far you'll be traveling, and being alone…" Hayland let the thought work its way through Cloud's mind.

"Our band lives near Bear Lake," he eventually replied. Bear Lake was almost three hours' ride away, and Hayland thought of the many dangers that the youth would have to face, not the least of which was the stagecoach riders looking for some sport on their way to California gold; or the soldiers from the nearby fort out on patrol, who had fought the Paiutes at the recent Pah Ute war.

The parting was awkward, the youth thankful but not wishing to be beholden to a white man by saying "thanks"; Hayland, sensing the unease of his young patient, decided against any outward indication of farewell.

"Be careful then."

Mounting his own horse, he and Cloud left the station, riding towards the creek where he had found him. Taking the bridle, he led the horse and rider across the rivulet. From there, they would find their way home safely.

There had been several times after that first encounter when Rushing Cloud had ridden in, shot his arrow, and they would meet at the river to conclude their business. On one of those meetings, he had brought a young Paiute woman with him, but it was not a workable suggestion, and the matter of a female companion had been laid to rest.

And now, this new summons. Hayland left the station along with his dog, who by then had become familiar with the routines of Rushing Cloud's visits. A full moon lit up the sky, throwing the surrounding trees into ghostly, looming shadows. The sounds of night critters scurrying in the underbrush had the dog tugging at the bit of rope in his master's hand, but a firm yank told him that this was not the time for hunting. An owl hooted, and the screech was like another piercing arrow in the stillness. Rushing Cloud was waiting, his mustang gelding standing quietly, for like the dog, he knew this routine well.

"Hi." The Indian spoke first.

Hayland nodded. "Got your arrows" he smiled in the dark, as he handed over the deadly weaponry. "What's the news?" he asked sharply.

"Not good," replied Rushing Cloud. "You'll have to come!"

"You know I can't do that," he stated flatly. He waved towards the station. "The riders, the horses they need." He stopped because even in the half light, he could see that it was not the answer that his young friend expected. Also, he would not have come so far if it were not serious. Instead, his voice grew soft as he asked,

"What is it?"

"We have one of your riders. He's in much pain!"

"When did this happen? And who has him? Where is he?" The questions now came fast as he tried to calm himself. Following the Pah Ute war a few months before in which many Indians were killed, the peace between the Plains people and the settlers was shaky, but at least the attacks were only sporadic and carried out by lone wolves. When the boy said that "we" have him, the word sent shivers through him.

"Two days ago," came the unsmiling reply. "He tried to escape, but our horses were fresher than his, and we caught him as he tried to cut across a low ridge."

"You said he's in pain. What happened?" prompted Hayland.

He liked his friend, but he hated his stilting communication skills.

Again, the Indian hesitated. He lowered his eyes and said, "There was a fight. He wouldn't give up his mochila, and they beat him and took it away." He paused again. "If I weren't there, he would be dead."

"How bad is he?" asked Hayland. "Any broken bones?" For the first time, there was a hint of jesting in his voice as he remembered that it was his broken leg that had made them friends.

"No, just the swelling from the beating. He groans a lot." He wiped his arm across his forehead, for the night was warm. The owl screeched again and flew noisily away to hunt.

"What are they planning to do to him?" he asked wistfully, for already a rescue plan was taking shape in his mind.

"We are waiting for him to heal, so that we can talk to him. I think they want to know how many horses are at the different stations so that, you know…" He left his answer at that for they both knew what the ending was.

"You said I had to go back with you. Why?"

"What d'you mean 'why'?" asked Rushing Cloud, surprised. "Isn't he your friend?"

"I don't know half of all the riders in the Express. One rider quits today, and a new one takes his place tomorrow. Happens all the time."

"Well, the truth is, he's been asking for you. He doesn't speak our language, and all he does is call your name. Any question we ask him gets the same reply."

Hayland knew, of course, that he would have to do what he could to save the boy, but only with an assurance that he'd be safe going into the Paiute camp.

When he had joined the Express, he had had to sign an oath, and at the time he had merely scanned the wording. But something had caught his attention. Near the end was a commitment that he would "…direct all [his] acts to win the confidence of [his] employers." This was a golden opportunity to do just that.

At swing-stations such as his, he had to be there when a rider came in to deposit his mochila, and deliver the one left by the last rider that rode in from the opposite direction.

His absence would cause no end of confusion and delay, as the riders would have to change the horses themselves. He was weighing the pros and cons when Cloud broke into his thoughts.

"He mightn't survive another day as he doesn't eat, and he cries all the time." There was a slight pause as the moon was suddenly darkened by a cloud rack. "He's just a boy. About my age."

"Will you help me to get him away?" No details; no pleading.

"Of course," came the immediate response.

It was this that settled it for Hayland. He would go to the Indians and bring back the young rider. The owners had made allowances for the rare times when, for instance, the station tender became ill and was unable to be about the compound. Until a temporary replacement could arrive at the station, a notice could be posted on a large notice board provided for that purpose.

"Wait for me," he said softly. In an instant he was gone, the Bluetick at this heels.

When he returned a half hour later, he was on one of the biggest horses they had for he might have to bring back both him and the kid. *It's a good thing that riders can't weigh more than a hundred and twenty pounds*, he thought.

The night got cool as they cantered along a well-worn path. There was little conversation, for voices carried far on still nights. They did not smoke either, for the same reason. By four o'clock they had reached the camp, and after notifying the chief of their return, Hayland and Cloud were taken to a tepee where they found the boy lying on a blanket on the ground. In the dim light of a dying wood fire, the youth rubbed his eyes trying to focus, and when he saw the American, he tried to rise, but the pain was too much.

"Hayland! I knew you'd come."

He knelt by the lad, felt his skin for a fever and was relieved that there was none.

"Listen to me," he spoke through his teeth. "I have a plan to get you away."

"What they saying?" asked one mean-looking Paiute warrior speaking to Rushing Cloud.

"He has white man's medicine to give the boy," Rushing Cloud replied, and without adding more turned away to avoid further questions.

The "medicine" that Hayland had brought was a bottle of pure creek water colored by a dark cough mixture. He also had a single velvet bean seed, a gift that he had received many years before by a trail rider from Louisiana. The hair that covered the pod caused immediate and uncontrollable itching when skin contact was made. Why he had kept it all this time he didn't know, and he wasn't sure that it would work. He had never tried it, of course. "And how do you stop the itching?" he had asked. "Just follow the cows; they leave it everywhere they go," was the wry reply.

"When I say drink, I want you to start coughing violently. Can you do that?" he asked the youth.

He nodded in response, and halfway through the dose, he began to cough. The warrior watched the process closely, but not close enough to see Hayland rub the seed into the lad's nape as he tilted his head for the last drop of the "medicine". The reaction was more than Hayland expected.

The boy began to tear at his hair and collar, writhing in discomfort from the itching. He screamed like a madman.

It took all three of them to restrain him long enough to tie him up. He screamed even louder, now that he was unable to rub the itch. A half dozen warriors appeared, but Rushing Cloud dismissed them, explaining that the medicine was too strong and that the boy might be losing his mind.

When the chief arrived, and Rushing Cloud had explained the situation to him, he agreed that Hayland should take the lad away, so that no babies born that day would hear the screams and grow to become like the wild boars.

Two weeks after that, Hayland heard a single arrow imbed itself in the wall. Cloud was waiting for him.

"How is the boy?" he asked.

"Much better. I took him to the Home Station in Guevarra near the fort."

Rushing Cloud smiled. "I saw what you did…with the seed. You're smart. Almost smart enough to be Paiute." Hayland remained silent; then he too smiled. They talked for a while after that.

"I'm glad you saved the boy. He was a distant cousin of the commander's wife. There would've been much bloodshed had he died."

They spoke some more, and as the moon began to rise, Rushing Cloud mounted and was about to ride off. "The woman, she asks for you. She's still alone. Like you. Goodnight, friend."

A month later, Hayland was made Station Head at Guevarra, with responsibility for nine swing stations.

He missed the old life but preferred the comforts of the new.

Acknowledgements

Thank you to Sue D. L. Smith for the front cover photo and to Chuck Baker for the back cover photo. In addition, many thanks are due to Mr. Leon Mixer who allowed us to use a photo of the front entrance of his ranch on our cover. We are also grateful to Cimarron Steakhouse of Oklahoma City for allowing us to use the picture by Sue D. L. Smith to grace the cover of this volume.

We also send thanks to Penny Beals and the El Reno Carnegie Library for their continued support and to the staff and administration of CVTech, the Canadian Valley Technology Center of El Reno/Yukon, who have hosted us these many semesters, allowing our writers and others to explore their publishing dreams.

In addition, we give much appreciation to our many beta-readers, who have helped proof and critique our writings before the final publishing. These include Barbara Foster of Okarche, Sheridan Marquardt of Oklahoma City, and John Aguilar of Bethany.

Thank you, everyone!

Editor Andrea Foster, leader of Creative Quills Writing Group, has been in the book business since 1977. She currently teaches Writing and Composition at Redlands Community College, Creative Writing at the Carnegie Library in El Reno OK and how to Write, Publish & Market Your Book at the Canadian Valley Technology Center, CVTech in El Reno/Yukon.

Foster began as an Op Ed writer for various newspapers in Connecticut and also did research and investigative reporting on such diverse subjects as government involvement in the arts, nuclear power plants, and toxic waste. She has written columns and articles for various magazines, newspapers, and websites and has several blogs.

She has given workshops for booksellers on how to create events and how to improve autographing events as well as seminars for authors at Writer's Conventions on how to get your book published and then market it.

Andrea's former lives include being Community Relations & Events Coordinator for Borders Books & Music, PR Queen working with authors as diverse as Captain Kangeroo and Kinky Friedman, and the **Regional Buyer** (New England & New York City) **for Waldenbooks** during the *SATANIC VERSES* era.

She has worked in every form of the media, including television and radio, mainly in and around the Houston area. **Andrea has a Bachelor's degree in Interpersonal Communications** and worked in the singles industry since 1996. She currently is a marketing consultant, teacher, professional counselor, and editor.

With over thirty years experience in the book business, including marketing and promotions, she has been interviewed on major networks about such controversial books as *SATANIC VERSES*, *AMERICAN PSYCHO*, and every book by the NRA's Wayne LaPierre.

Other Books by Creative Quills:

Alternate Perspectives

Upcoming Books:

Tales from Childhood

Modern Day Myths

Horror Stories

Websites:

http://www.creativequills.com
http://www.okwriters.com
http://www.writeok.com
http://www.meetup.com/CreativeQuills/
http://www.thebooklady.info

Cacti and Wagon Wheel with Cart
by Sue D. L. Smith

Photo by Chuck Baker of the Mixer Ranch

Happy Tales & Trails to You All!